I0684650

Return To Oli's Gold

Cousins coming of age on the
19th century frontier

Book Three

James Oliver Virmala

Edition 2

Cover Photo By Randy and Mary
Smith

ISBN: 13: 978-0-9972536-2-7

ACKNOWLEDGEMENT

To Barb and Bill, dear friends and mentors on my books.

BOOKS BY THE AUTHOR

Oli's Gold Book One
Search For Oli's Gold Book Two
Return To Oli's Gold Book Three
To Be A Mountain Man
Trouble On The Kansas Plains
Frontier Justice
Return Of The Mountain Man
The Tall Man
The Prospector
The Green Valley
Twilight Of The Mountain Man
The Mother Lode
Quest Of The Mountain Man
Journey's End
Rufus Pike
Rufus And The Pup
The Winding Trail Home
Rufus The Lost Years
The Kankakee Kid
Bogus Island
Tyler Tomas The Brothers' War

CONTENTS

RETURN TO OLI'S GOLD

CHAPTER ONE

The sound of children playing came from behind the small house on Turkey River. The sun was shining and the sky was blue, with the occasional fluffy white cloud. It was July 4, 1889. Long tables with benches were set up in the yard. The table was heaped with plates of fried chicken, potato salad, fresh corn, fresh peas, corn bread, and pitchers of sweet iced tea.

The weathered log house had two stories and a long porch on the river side. The barn and workshop were just north of the house. The hip roof barn had a large opening in the center, to allow loads of hay to be pulled in and then pitched into the loft. The workshop was painted red, with white trim. It had once been the place of employment for grandfather Oli and had proudly bore a sign that said:

RETURN TO OLI'S GOLD

Oli's Repair Shop
No Job Too Small
Some Too Big

The sign was now stored in the attic of the shop, which was no longer used for business. Tools were kept there to fix broken items around the farm. There was a wooden workbench in the middle of the room. Shelves lined the walls and a potbelly stove provided heat in the winter.

One of the shelves was left undisturbed from the time Oli had made his livelihood. It had four small wooden boxes containing flint, tinder, and striking steel. The boxes showed their age, but were kept dusted and ready if needed. Every time the family looked at them, they could remember Oli's stories of wandering in the wilderness without fire.

It was also a favorite place for Oli's three sons, Karl, Tony and Haat, or their boys, Vic, Dan, and Zac. They would meet there to plan adventures. There were handmade wooden stools around the workbench. An old, blackened coffee pot sat on the potbelly stove.

On this sunny Independence Day, children ran around playing tag. Two young girls near the river were being scolded for playing in the mud. Everyone was back from the parade. Elkader, Iowa was proud of the celebration it put on. The streets were decorated with flags and bunting. There were horse races, draft horse pulls, and a dance coming up later in the day.

The three middle-aged August brothers sat near the old workshop, sharing a pail of beer and watching their sons competing throwing knives against a board leaning against the wall.

"They're pretty darn good, Tony," Karl said. Karl August had blond hair with just a bit of gray in the temples. He had a thick, bushy moustache, which he liked to curl. His blue eyes twinkled as he watched the boys with pride. He and Karen lived at the home with his mother, Joan.

Karl's son was Victor. He was named after Karl's grandfather. Vic had broad shoulders and a narrow waist. He had his father's blue eyes. His Grandma Joan said he was an image of Karl's father, Oli. Vic had just turned 20. All he talked about was going west someday.

"Do you think Daniel is ready for the Good Knife?" Tony asked Karl.

Tony was referring to the knife passed down to him from their father, Oli. It had been modified for throwing by a man whom Oli had met on the wagon train while traveling west. He had called it the 'Good Knife'. The Good Knife itself had been the difference between surviving or dying during

Oli's adventure in the wilderness 50 years earlier.

Tony August had become a little stocky with age and had short, brown hair. Everyone blamed Tony's weight on Ruth's good cooking. They had built a house within easy walking distance of the home. Tony had a quick wit and was by far the best with a knife.

Dan was Tony and Ruth's son. He was named after his mother's father. Ruth's father and family had been killed by renegade confederate soldiers in Oklahoma. Dan had curly, brown hair and gray eyes. He was tall and thin, with slightly stooped shoulders and narrow hips. He sported a Colt .44 on his hip. He had won the handgun quick draw earlier that day. He drew and knocked three cans off the rail before the bell. Normally, he didn't walk around town with a gun, but he hadn't had a chance to take it off yet. Dan August was 22 years-old.

"I don't know about you, brothers, but my Zac is the best with a knife," Haat said. "The Good Knife should go to the best arm." Haat August had a Ho-Chunk mother and Oli August was his father. His hair was streaked with gray. He wore it long in a loose braid. His creased face was the result of much laughter and too much time in the sun. Haat's brown eyes appraised his son's ability and he could not have been more proud.

Zac's first name came from the Ho-chunk word nązazáč, which translates to "branch of tree". He had the family's last name, August, out of respect for his grandfather, Oli August. Zac was 21 years-old, average height, and lean. His strength far surpassed his size. His father had taught Zac the ways of their tribe the Ho-Chunk, better known as the Winnebago. Zac had spent many hours in the saddle, and could ride just about anything with hair.

"It's time to eat. Put those knives and that gun away, and pull up a bench," Jenny said.

She then sent her husband, Albert Keller, to get the younger children. Jenny was Karl's and Tony's sister. She and Albert had six children. They had waited to start a family until Albert got his own grist mill running. After that, no time was wasted having a brood. Jenny had a round face and a few extra pounds. Her hair had darkened over the years and had a bit more red than blond. She still had the freckles across her cheeks and smiling hazel eyes.

Two white-haired ladies sat on a glider swing under a large oak tree. They enjoyed watching the young people. Joan August had a fair complexion and Nina had a darker complexion from her Ho-Chunk heritage. Joan and Nina had become good friends after Oli's death.

Nina's   Ho-Chunk   name   was

Huhawira-Nina, which translated to moon on the water. She now went by Nina, the name Oli had called her.

They had shared the same man in two different eras of his life. Oli had met and lost Nina during his trip through the wilderness. He had never known of his son Haat. Joan had met Oli right here on the banks of Turkey River. He had walked out of the river wearing rags, with hair that made him look like a wild man. She had loaned him a flint to start a fire.

When Oli had been accused of attacking the Wolfe brothers after he had emerged from the Turkey River, Joan had come to his defense, preventing him from a 30-day stay in the local jail. After a short courtship the two were married and made their home in the two-room workshop, which was the first building Oli had built on the banks of the river. They had raised three children: Karl, Tony, and Jenny.

After the three brothers had met during the search for their father's hidden gold, Karl and Tony told Joan about Nina and Haat. It had been her wish to meet the rest of her husband's family. Nina and Haat, with his wife Carol, moved to Elkader. They had built a house next to Joan, on the site where the burning house had killed Oli as he was rescuing a young girl. They had shared stories of Oli with tears and laughter.

More than one evening would find the grandmothers, Joan and Nina, sitting in the workshop, drinking coffee. Joan had hung the weathered deerskin coat, which looked more like a vest, on a peg. It would remind them of the man they had known.

Karen, Karl's wife, was putting pies on one of the tables. She watched Haat and his son Zac walk toward the table, poking and kidding each other. She thought back to 10 years ago, when Haat's wife Carol became ill with an infected appendix. She had died with her husband and son by her side. It took several years before Haat was able to laugh freely. It made her feel good watching them having fun.

Dan, Vic, and Zac sat together at the table with their fathers. They talked excitedly about going west and becoming ranchers. They had planned to try and get some land in the Oklahoma land rush the past April. Karl and Tony had a sawmill and had just received a large government order. The boys were working for them and they couldn't be spared.

They were able to convince the boys that the land rush was for farmers and not ranchers. The three finally understood, but the desire to ride the rails to the west was mighty strong.

CHAPTER TWO

Tony had just sat down from saying grace when gunshots were heard. They looked toward the town and could hear shouting.

"They robbed the bank! Stop them, they robbed the bank!"

The three men and their sons ran toward the noise. Dan ran past the house to grab his gun. Four robbers rode by, firing at random, leaving the pursuing town folk behind. One of the bullets shattered a front window pane in the workshop.

They arrived at the dirt road with the dust of the departing horses drifting over them. Dan ran up, holding his Colt, searching for a target. Several men from the town ran up and stopped in front of them, staring in the direction that the robbers had gone.

A stocky man with arms that bulged in his shirt turned to Karl. "The sons-of-bitches shot and wounded the sheriff!" The man was Gus Beckmann, the town's blacksmith.

"How is the sheriff?" Karl asked.

RETURN TO OLI'S GOLD

A bald, slender man with a thin moustache named George Walters, owner of the mercantile, answered Karl's question.

"He will be okay, but he won't be able to go after the bank robbers."

The group hurried back to the scene of the crime. Paul Blevins, the banker, was standing on the steps.

"I tell you," he said, "the bank will pay $1,000 reward for the return of the money."

"How about the robbers?" a stocky farmer, in for the celebration, asked.

Paul Blevins' face was red and his eyes were blazing. He turned to the stocky farmer. "I don't give a damn what happens to the four robbers. I do not think they should ever be seen again. The reward is for the return of the money."

Haat turned to his brothers. "Someone said it's the Alan gang. The Alans tend to shoot and then ask questions."

Tony nodded. "They are darn loose with the gun. You notice they weren't hitting anything on the way out of town."

"Or were they hitting everything they wanted?" Karl asked.

The crowd began to disperse. Most headed back to their picnics, a few headed for the tavern. Nobody stood up and offered to go after the Alans. The banker estimated that they had gotten away with just over $20,000. A part of that was in the town's account for completing the Keystone Bridge across the Turkey River.

Karl knew that they had their sawmill payroll at the bank, plus other money for day-to-day business. Tony had just deposited their receipts the day before. The deposits were not guaranteed and if the robbery caused Paul Blevins to close the bank, the money would be lost.

The brothers had a safety stash hidden in a small safe at Karl's. It was probably enough to keep them going. The extra had come from the government contract that Karen's uncle had helped them get. Major Thomas was now retired but still had helpful connections.

The ladies had let the children finish eating and did their best to keep the flies away from the food. It was no longer fresh when they returned, but none of the men or boys complained. They were busy answering the ladies' questions as they ate.

The robbery had put a damper on the afternoon celebration. By the time the dance began, spirits seemed to be picking up. Vic and Dan were anxious to get to the dance. They had been spending time with the Schmidt sisters, Marie and Mary. Zac tagged along, looking forward to getting some dancing in.

Chairs were brought out to the porch, and the rest of the family sat to enjoy the evening breeze. Jenny motioned to Albert. They collected their children and headed home. The two youngest ones were asleep in their arms.

Joan sat looking at the Turkey River. She could still envision Oli the first time she saw him, standing on the bank dripping from waist down, dressed in ragged clothes. She began to softly sing one of the Finnish lullabies that he had taught her.

Karen and Ruth turned to face the three brothers. Each had a long cigar and they were competing blowing smoke rings.

"You know the boys want to go after the Alan gang," Karen said.

Ruth brushed some crumbs from her apron. "You can't let them go. I lost a family once. I couldn't do it again."

The brothers knew better than to say anything about the subject. They had heard the boys planning their search. The reason for going to the dance was to tell their girlfriends goodbye. Time had already been spent in the workshop putting their gear together.

Joan and Nina sat quietly, listening to the wives. "You best plan on spending extra time in church praying for the boys' safety," Joan advised.

Nina sat looking into the dark. She was thinking of her cousin who had tried to kill Oli. They had wanted to make sure Oli didn't follow Nina and it had cost her cousin his life. "The boys have good judgment. If they go, they will remember that they have families and that the families need them to come back."

Ruth let out a small cry of protest and then began to weep. Karen put her arm around Ruth's shoulder.

"We knew they would go," Karen whispered. "Someone has to make the Alan gang responsible for what they did."

Tired from the day's activities, Ruth called to their daughters, Sarah and Rebecca. The girls loved sitting by the river. After quick hugs all around, the girls led the way toward their house.

The boys came back home late. Grandma Joan's was a favorite place to go, they often spent the night in the upstairs bedrooms. Everyone but their Grandma had gone to bed.

"What time do you plan to leave?" she inquired.

"Early," Vic replied.

"The Alans have a 20-hour lead on us," Dan said, "but we don't think they traveled too far. Without immediate pursuit, we think they'll hold up to plan their next move."

Joan put some molasses cookies and cold milk out for them. The three cousins sat around the kitchen table, eating cookies and telling her about the dance. Joan wanted the time with the boys. She knew when men went out to hunt other men, the results are not always good. She hoped they were going after the Alan gang to make things right and not for the reward.

CHAPTER THREE

The three cousins sat tall in their saddles while saying goodbye to the family. Karl was proud of how they looked. They all had dark pants tucked into high-topped boots. They wore solid color shirts made of light wool. The fathers had bought each of them Winchester Model 1873 rifles as a bonus for staying around to help and not go to the Oklahoma land rush. Each cousin was also armed with Colt .44 handguns.

Vic wore a flat-brimmed hat with a round crown. He had a knife sheathed on his left hip and the Colt with white ivory grips holstered on his right. He rode a long-legged black gelding with a white blaze on its forehead.

Dan liked the traditional cowboy hat, with its curved brim and creased crown. He carried a knife in the top of his boot and wore a Colt with black mahogany grips on his left hip. He rode a buckskin with a little darker mane than the one his Uncle Karl had.

Zac sat loosely in the saddle. He wore a flat-brimmed hat with a flat crown. His Uncle Tony walked up to his sorrel. Reaching behind his neck, he handed Zac the Good Knife.

"You have earned this. You have a good eye and a quick hand with a knife."

Zac took the knife and replaced the one on the nape of his neck with the Good Knife. A round of applause rose from the others. The Good Knife had a new owner.

Feeling a bit awkward, Zac adjusted his Colt with light brown grips on his right hip. The sorrel sensed his owner's emotion and danced around, the morning sun highlighting its three white stockings.

Their grandmothers, Joan and Nina, had provided them with food that should last them a week. These were packed in the saddlebags, along with extra .44 cartridges and other necessary odds and ends.

Ruth reached up to hold Dan's hands as they got ready to ride out.

"I expect you to be back home by the end of the week. Your sisters don't want to keep doing your chores," she said with a forced smile.

The three cousins rode their horses to

the outskirts of town. They had scouted the trail the afternoon before to make sure they had the direction before the tracks were covered by departing July 4th celebrators.

Zac was the best tracker and led the group. Karl watched them go. He knew the fathers should be with the sons. Their business wouldn't allow it. After they had returned with their father's gold and were married, a sawmill came on the market and Karl and Tony had purchased it. Later, when Haat and his mother moved to Elkader, he bought a share.

They had 25 people working at the mill, depending on them. It would not have been right to go on a chase that could take several weeks.

The July sun was hot on their backs as they followed the tracks west. Zac stayed on the trail while Vic and Dan spread out to each side, watching the horizon. They were riding across a grassy plain with wildflowers splashing orange, purple and yellow colors across the rolling hills. Birds and butterflies were everywhere. They came to a wagon trail and a killdeer ran in front of them, dragging a wing and faking an injury to draw them away from the nest.

Zac held up his hand to stop the others. They moved slowly to Zac, watching the area around them. The wagon trail meandered around the hills and disappeared on a knoll about a half mile away. It went behind a clump of aspen and two large ash trees.

"One of the horses is having a problem," Zac said, pointing to the shoe tracks. "It's favoring a front hoof."

Zac swung down and looked at the track closer. Once they started following a track, they were able to identify characteristics of the hooves and shoes. They were like a signature confirming that they were on the right trail. The trail had been easy to follow, showing the arrogance of the robbers. They had been traveling fast, while not taking any measures to cover their back trail.

"It's losing a shoe. The rider won't get far on this horse. They will need another, so we need to be careful, and travel slower for a while." Zac swung back into the saddle.

The three spread out and continued toward the knoll. Dan rode slowly, straining his eyes, searching the hills for any sign of the riders. He was the oldest cousin and the others had always looked up to him. For the first time he felt vulnerable, expecting a bullet anytime.

He wondered if Zac felt the same. He looked so confident, with his high cheek bones and his eyes squinting at the trail. Never had he seen a man as comfortable in a saddle. He could tell Vic was nervous. He had a habit of glancing quickly to the right and left when trouble came.

Zac dismounted and walked beside his horse, using it as a shield as they moved toward the trees. Vic and Dan spread out wider, attempting to make themselves a less inviting target. They did not know if the Alan gang was holed up on the knoll, but they were sure that it was their destination.

Vic was moving around the left side of the knoll when he suddenly waved to the others. He had found the trail leaving the trees. Zac rode up and looked at the tracks.

"They are riding three horses. One is doubled up. They are leading the fourth horse. These tracks are less than six hours old."

Dan looked at the tracks and agreed with Zac. Growing up and spending hours on the prairie and in the woods with their fathers, they had made tracking and hunting a game. Much time had been spent teaching the boys how to choose and set up a proper camp. They would split up and one group would leave after breakfast. The rest would track them, with the objective of arriving at the new camp in time for supper.

Survival camping had often been done. They would be dropped off by their fathers with a knife and flint. They'd carried a pack with enough food for two days. The objective had been to catch up with their fathers after a four-day hike and have their original food left.

They'd made their own bows and arrows and gone hunting around Turkey River, often bringing home meat for supper.

Moving carefully, the three rode toward the trees. They were confident that the knoll held no danger, but a little caution did not hurt.

The robbers' camp showed evidence of being quickly set up and abandoned. The fire still had some warmth in the coals. The cousins knew better than to leave hot embers behind.

Vic shook his head and knelt to make a small fire so they could have coffee before continuing. "They really don't care about anything or anyone but themselves," he said.

Dan called out, "Look here. They left some bloody bandages. The sheriff must have hit one of them."

While the coffee water came to a boil, the three of them looked off in the direction the men had gone.

"I think they will head for the Fayette Road to get another horse," Zac surmised. "We can gain time if we keep more westerly."

"If they decide to turn south, we will lose time," Dan said, "but I agree with Zac. I think they will head toward Fayette after they get another horse."

"Why don't we split? Dan and I can ride to cut them off. Zac, you follow the tracks in case they turn off. We will backtrack along the Fayette Road and meet up with you," Vic suggested.

Little discussion was done while they quickly had something to eat. The cousins had a plan and it was time to move. Clouds were building to the west and it promised the coming of a storm. Once the rain started, tracking would be very difficult. They made sure that the fire was out before getting their horses.

Zac left first, following the tracks.

"Don't take any chances," Dan warned.

Zac smiled and waved. He rode hard in the direction of the gang. He glanced back and saw Vic and Dan ride off toward the Fayette Road.

They had about six more hours of daylight and had every intention of using it all. Zac rode a little east of the tracks as he approached the Fayette Road. He didn't want to come up on the Alans unexpectedly. The road followed a stream and had several groups of trees, which would make good cover for someone wanting to ambush a rider.

Zac could ride a little faster, knowing his quarry had an objective and it would be unlikely they would stop before reaching it. He did find an area where they had rested the horses. They had switched the horse that was riding double.

Arriving at the road east of the trail,

Zac estimated that the Alans would intercept the road about three miles further west. Calling it a road was a stretch. It was more like two ruts cut into the prairie sod.

Now he rode with care. Zac watched the road ahead for any sign of the men. The Fayette Road was not a highly travelled road. He knew that unless they were lucky they would have quite a wait for a rider and horse.

The sun was getting low in the sky. He was riding west and the long shadows made it hard to pick out a man waiting. Zac pulled his horse over to the side of the road and settled down to have a cold meal of sliced beef and bread, while waiting for the sun to slide behind the horizon. He drank from his canteen to wash down the food.

After sunset, he continued up the road, leading his sorrel. The moon came up bright in the east. He knew that once the clouds came over, it would be too dark to pick up any sign.

Zac stopped suddenly. He could see something move up the road. Tying the sorrel to a low bush, he continued staying close to any available cover. He could make out a horse standing just off the road. It was pulling at the grass and favored one leg when it moved.

He searched the area for any other movement. His eyes picked up a form, lying in one of the ruts of the road. He crept forward for a better look. It was a body.

Zac went back for his horse and led it toward the dead man. A quick investigation determined that the man had been shot in the back. Slowly, Zac looked the area over. With the help of the moonlight and careful probing fingers, he put the scene together.

The Alan gang had staked the lame horse out on the road. They then waited off the road, near the stream, for an unfortunate rider to come along. When the rider went to check on the horse, he had been shot in the back.

A chill went down Zac's spine. They were dealing with cold-blooded killers who held little value for life. He glanced up the road with worry for his cousins. He decided that little could be done for the poor chap that they had killed, and he had to keep moving.

He checked the lame horse. The shoe was now completely off. He tied the body to the back of the horse with a note of explanation. Zac pulled up the picket and then he slapped it on the rump, sending it east down the road. Zac hoped someone would find the horse and give the man a proper burial.

With the benefit of a full moon and the threat of rain clouds in the near future, Zac decided to keep after the Alan gang. He was sure they would continue toward the town of Fayette. He had also found where one of the wounded gang members had laid during the ambush. They had made him a bed of cedar branches and Zac had found blood. Based on how the man was laying, it appeared that the wound was low on his right side. Zac turned his horse west after the gang.

* * *

Dan and Vic cut toward the Fayette Road. The road followed a stream that swung south in a big curve. By cutting directly west they could save several miles and, with luck, would be ahead of the gang.

They watched the clouds building in front of them. They kept their horses at a mile- eating trot. It was just after sunset when they reached the road. They searched for any new tracks in the fading light. They found none. The moon was coming up, and bathed the road in soft light. Dan looked at the parallel ruts winding along the stream and wondered how far back the Alan gang was. He had an agonizing fear that the robbers would leave the road and strike south.

Dan and Vic decided to ride east for another hour. At the same time, they would look for a good spot to lay and wait for the gang. The night was alive with the sound of frogs and crickets. An owl complained in the dark, while coyotes yapped and howled as they chased some prey.

The clopping of the horses and the

creak of their saddles was the only noise Dan and Vic added to the night. They had removed their spurs and put them into their saddlebags. This would prevent the jingle while sneaking up on the bad guys.

Dan turned and rode up a rise. He sat looking east. After a couple of minutes, he rode back down and joined Vic.

"I didn't see any sign of a fire. I will feel much better when we have them spotted. Until that happens, we could draw unexpected gunfire at any time," Dan said.

"This isn't quite like I thought it would be," Vic confided. "When we go hunting game, they don't shoot back. I hadn't figured on that back in town."

Dan knew if he told his cousin it was okay to stay back, he would not. Vic was just telling him how he felt. Yet he knew what he had to do.

After 45 minutes of riding, they saw a tree-covered hill. It overlooked the road and would give them cover. Dan guided his black up the hill. There was a windfall at the crest that was ideal for cover. Vic started setting up their camp, moving some of the fallen branches and piling them between the road and their camp. Dan moved the horses further back into the trees and picketed them on a patch of grass.

Dan and Vic decided they would take two-hour shifts watching the road. Dan took the first watch. The night was quiet, except for frogs. Their peeping was a soothing sound.

It was an hour before sunrise and there was a soft rain falling. Dan had finished his second watch and went to wake Vic. They were sleeping under a large, old rock maple, and its leaves gave them some protection from the rain.

Just as he reached to wake Vic, he heard a gunshot. Vic rolled out of his covers and began to pull his boots on. Within minutes, they had their horses saddled and were riding east. They began to hear sporadic gunshots.

* * *

Zac had been riding most of the night. The rain had just begun to fall when he heard somebody cry out. Someone ahead of him was in pain.

Swinging down from his horse, Zac moved toward the sound. His horse was trained to stop when the reins were dropped. Crouching in the soft rain, Zac strained his ears to get a line on their camp. He heard a horse snort to his right. Again, he heard a groan ahead of him.

With the help of the damp ground, Zac moved soundlessly through the trees to the horses. Speaking softly to them to prevent any nickering, he released them, one at a time. As quietly as possible, he herded the horses away from the robbers' camp.

He figured that he had gotten away with it when the sound of a cocking gun reached his ears. Zac threw himself forward as the bullet passed just over his head and the crash of the gunshot echoed in the trees.

Zac landed on the ground and rolled left. Then, on his hands and knees, he crawled through the brush looking for something to hide behind. He heard another searching shot and knew that the shooter didn't know where he was.

Circling around, Zac headed for this horse. While they looked for him, he did not want them to find his horse. He wouldn't put it past them to shoot it out of pure meanness.

Dan and Vic rode blindly through the night, the rain stinging their faces. Vic saw a muzzle flash in front of them and felt a bullet burn across the top of his shoulder. He felt himself falling backward over the horse's rump. He kicked wildly to get his toes out of the stirrups.

Vic landed on his back. He lay there, unable to move or breathe. Hitting the ground had knocked the wind out of him. He was sure his problem was because he had been shot. He could hear the horses running away. Suddenly, he pulled in a ragged breath. Dirt hit the side of his face from another shot.

No longer feeling immobile, Vic

scrambled off the road into some briar bushes. The thorns tore at his clothes and buried in his hands as he crawled down what appeared to be an animal path. He emerged out the other side of the briars and came face-to-face with a huge, wide-faced robber with a gun in his right hand. Both were shocked to see the other. Vic, being the quicker of the two, lunged forward, tackling the man.

He could hear gunfire all around him, and he did his best to hang on to the robber. It felt like he had grabbed a wild bull. Vic knew that if the man broke his grip and threw him off, he would swing the gun around and shoot him. Vic's gun was still in his holster with the loop holding it secure, too secure.

The man stood up, dragging Vic with him. He was trying to beat Vic with his gun barrel. Vic stomped down on his instep and then brought his knee up into his groin. The big man howled and fell to the ground, pulling Vic with him. Vic found himself looking down on the man. He was looking into the wildest eyes he had ever seen.

Poking his fingers into the man's eyes, Vic threw himself clear. Rolling over, he grabbed at his revolver. The big man was rubbing his eyes as Vic's gun came up. Vic noticed that the man did not have a gun in either hand. The lug had dropped it. The man turned to jump toward Vic and stared into the barrel of Vic's six-shooter.

He froze and cried out, "Don't shoot me, please don't shoot me."

Vic heard a shot and the big man's throat exploded, showering Vic with blood and tissue. The big man then fell on top of him. Vic looked for the shooter, while trying to pull his gun free. The shooter was one of the Alans! He was swinging his gun in line with Vic when a shot from the direction of the road shattered the shooter's elbow. The gun fell from numbed fingers and he grabbed his shattered arm.

For a moment all was quiet. Vic then heard Dan shouting his name. "Vic, are you okay? Vic!"

"I am over here, Dan!" Vic hollered back. "Come and help me with this mountain of a man."

"Are you both okay?" It was Zac. He was pushing one of the robbers in front of him.

The man had several cuts and what appeared to be a broken nose, based on the amount of blood running down his face. Zac had a long cut across his chest, which was soaking his wool shirt with blood.

With Dan's help, Vic rolled the big man off him. He was splattered with the man's blood. His mouth had been open when the bullet hit the big man and some of the blood had sprayed into it. Vic got to his knees before nausea swept over him and he began to retch violently.

Zac had his gun on the two standing robbers. They were the Alan brothers, Sid and Len. Sid was the one who'd fought with Zac. Len stood holding his broken arm, looking pale and sick.

Zac heard a horse coming up behind him, drew his revolver and swung it to bear on the approaching rider. He chuckled when he saw the lame horse with the unfortunate man tied to its back. The horse evidently didn't want to be left alone and had followed Zac.

After making sure that his cousin had no wounds that needed attention, Dan looked around and found the fourth wounded robber. The smell of his festered wound made Dan's stomach turn. The man was unaware and burning up with fever. His breathing was ragged. Dan doubted he would last the day.

The sun came up. The rain stopped, but mist and fog shrouded the landscape. Large drops continued to fall from the trees.

Zac tied Sid Alan with leather string from their saddlebag. Dan worked on Len Alan, trying to staunch the bleeding and immobilize the arm using makeshift splints. Vic was down by the stream, stripped naked, washing himself and his clothes.

Vic came back from the stream wearing his wet pants. He hadn't put on his shirt yet.

"Dan, can you check my shoulder? I was hit by a bullet. It stings like crazy," he said, trying to turn his head to see the cut.

"Come here and let me see," Dan said, motioning him over. "If you were shot, you best not complain to your mother. She would never let you away from town again."

Zac had the two Alan brothers bound and secured to an aspen tree. He then got his horse.

"I'll go up to your camp and bring the rest of your stuff back here."

Zac needed to get away from the scene of the fight for a moment. Once he was relaxed, he felt a weakness in his legs. He was also exhausted having ridden all night.

As he rode toward his cousin's camp, his mind played back the fight. After he had gotten away from Sid Alan, Zac had gone to get his horse. He had just gotten there when Sid loomed out of the dark. He'd held a six shooter in his hand. Again, Zac had thrown himself out of the line of the bullet. He'd leaped back toward Sid, ducking under his outstretched gun.

Sid had been searching the darkness, expecting Zac to run away. His attack had been unexpected. Sid and Zac had gone down in a heap and had wrestled briefly on the side of the road. They'd broken loose from each other. Sid had come up with his knife in his hand. Evidently, he'd lost the grip on his gun when tackled. Zac had reached for his gun and the holster was empty. He had pulled the

Good Knife from its sheath.

His first instinct had been to throw the knife. He had changed his mind quickly. If by chance the throw had only wounded Sid, he would be unarmed. Slowly, they had circled each other. Sid had thought himself an expert with the knife and had had a vicious smile on his face.

"I am going to take you apart, piece by piece," he had snarled.

As they'd circled, each had feigned a swipe at the other, testing their opponent's quickness. Zac's ankle had turned in the rut in the road and he'd stumbled. Sid had closed and had barely caught Zac with the slashing maneuver. Zac had felt the knife slice across his chest, drawing blood. He'd stepped back and right, narrowly avoided Sid's lunge to end the fight. Zac had stuck out his foot and had tripped Sid. Sid's forward momentum had carried him past Zac and he'd hit the ground, done an expert roll, and had been back on his feet, facing Zac with his knife up.

Zac had been impressed with Sid's agility and only wished he'd had time to appreciate it. Facing each other, they had started to circle again when the shooting had begun on the far side of the camp.

"Your friends are dying right now," Sid had laughed. "Drop the knife, and I will let you bury them before I kill you."

Zac had felt the sting as his sweat

seeped into the cut on his chest. Right then, he hadn't time to think about Dan and Vic. He had hoped that Sid was wrong. All of a sudden, Sid lunged. Zac had side stepped and had captured Sid's arm under his. He had then flattened Sid's nose with the butt end of the Good Knife.

He'd pushed Sid back and had slashed at him, which had cut Sid's cheek from ear to chin. Sid had been temporarily blinded from tears caused by the crushed nose. Zac had kicked the wrist of Sid's knife hand and had sent the weapon flying.

Spinning Sid around, Zac had laid the Good Knife blade across Sid's throat. "Had enough, mister?"

"I'm through. Where the hell did you learn to fight with a knife?"

It was then that Zac had felt an object under his foot. He had pushed Sid ahead and reached down, finding his Colt .44.

Reliving the fight, Zac had been riding blindly, when he realized that he'd arrived at the cousins' camp. The memories had raised his adrenalin a bit and made him feel a bit better. Zac was now happy that he had spent the long hours with his father practicing knife fighting. It was his father who had taught him not to throw a knife during a fight. Once thrown, your defense was gone.

He found Dan's and Vic's blankets. They were soaking wet. He chuckled, knowing that they had at least two days ride back to Elkader. They would be most uncomfortable sleeping. Quickly collecting their stuff, Zac rode back to the robbers' camp. Dan walked up to get the gear and bring Zac up to date.

"The wounded robber's name was Ron. He just died. The other gang member who was shot by Len Alan was named Pete. When he had surrendered to Vic, Len shot him. He didn't like cowards."

Vic came back into camp, leading the Alan gang's horses.

"They didn't wander too far when you let them go, Zac," he said glancing at the lame horse. "I don't think I have ever seen horses that wanted to stay as close as these."

Laughing, Vic led the horses toward the picket line. Dan was glad, to see that his cousin was in better spirits. When he ran toward the stream to wash Pete's blood off himself and his clothes, Dan was worried how it would affect him.

Zac looked around the camp. Dan had a fire going and some coffee boiling. He could see that Dan was just about to start slicing bacon into a black frying pan.

"Could you save me some bacon and biscuits? Some coffee would be good, too. I want to sleep for a couple of hours first. I rode all night, and am tired enough to sleep standing up."

"Curl up for a couple of hours, Zac. We'll have chow ready when you wake up. We will also get the bodies ready to travel," Dan said. "Oh, and we found the bank money."

Vic walked up after tying the horses. "I would put some pine pitch and spider webs on that chest cut before you go to sleep," he advised.

CHAPTER FOUR

The ride back to Elkader was without incident. The dead had no complaints. Len whined about his arm and moaned every time the horse jarred him. Sid required watching. His eyes were wild and he threatened the cousins with every kind of pain, all the way back.

The town cheered their arrival with the money. The sheriff, Alvin Wallace, was back at work, supporting a large bandage on his neck.

"Would have killed me if it was an inch over," he said, pointing to the bandage.

He took charge of Sid and Len Alan. The doctor was called to check their injuries.

The banker, Paul Blevins, welcomed the cousins back with open arms, assured them that the $1,000 would be paid. Once the money was in his hands, he quickly forgot about the boys and headed into his bank. The rest of the town did not forget and there was quite the celebration that night. Marie and Mary stayed close to Vic and Dan all evening. Zac was busy dancing, much in demand.

Morning found Vic sitting on the porch, drinking hot black coffee. His head had just about quit aching from the celebration the night before. His father, Karl, had already gone to work at the sawmill. He could hear his mother taking care of the morning dishes. His Grandma Joan joined him on the porch. She sat in the rocker next to Vic.

"Had a good time last night?" she inquired.

"Too good, Grandma. Marie stuck to me all night and everyone wanted to keep buying drinks."

"You like Marie?" she teased.

"Why is it that girls think they own you? I could have danced with all kinds of good-looking girls last night. An opportunity like that doesn't come by too often. But no chance. Marie stuck by me like glue."

Joan looked at her grandson. It was evident that he wasn't ready to settle down yet. His father had tried to get him to go east to college, but all he dreamt of was having a ranch out west.

"You know, Victor, there will come a

time when you'll meet a girl you will want to stick close to. You should be flattered that she likes you so much," she said.

"I think the town thought of us as some kind of heroes. I think she liked the attention of being with a hero. If it had been someone else, she would have been with him."

Smiling, she leaned back in the rocker and watched an eagle swoop down and snatch a fish out of the river. Victor was a smart young man, she thought.

Zac walked over from next door and sat on the edge of the porch. He had brought his whetstone and was working on the edge of the Good Knife.

"We will have to go to court when the Alans go on trial," he said to Vic.

"I imagine we will," Vic replied. "I figure they should both hang."

"Grandma Joan, Grandma Nina wants you to join her in town today," Zac said. "She mentioned something about a hat sale."

Joan nodded. Summer mornings, and small talk, that's what makes a family. She wished her Oli would have been here to see this.

The same warming sun was shining on a small two-story house located on a tree-lined Elkader side street. Dan walked out of the house, grabbing a ginger cookie. "I have to go and see Zac and Vic. I will be back for dinner."

Ruth looked at her son. His curly

brown hair reminded her of her father. "Ask Karen if they have plans for the weekend."

Dan trotted down the lane toward the workshop. Zac and Vic had found something in an out-of-town paper that they wanted to talk to him about.

He walked into the shop and stopped for a moment. He always liked the smell of the workshop. The smell of leather, saddle soap, grease, and metal filings filled his nostrils. It made him closer to his grandfather. He enjoyed listening to his father and uncles talking about his grandfather's adventure in the wilderness.

"Get over here and look at this," Vic said excitedly.

Zac moved the newspaper toward Dan. He saw the ad in the middle of the classified page.

Wanted
Drovers needed to
move large herd
from New Mexico
to Wyoming. If
qualified contact:
Bill Tilison –
Flying T Ranch,
Kansas City, MO

Dan looked at the date of the newspaper. It was only two weeks old. He looked at the smiling cousins.

"We always talk about going out west. If we could hire on with this outfit, we would have an objective and a chance to make some money. Our families couldn't say no," Vic gushed.

Zac was thoughtful. "Our fathers did make a cattle drive to save grandma's home. We all worked on the Taylor ranch for two summers. We can ask Mr. Taylor to write a reference for us."

Dan chuckled. "Don't be too sure about a reference. We worked days and chased his daughters at night. We may not have left on the best of terms the last summer we worked."

He remembered old man Taylor catching them with his daughters in the hayloft. Even though they were being proper with the girls, it had the appearance of something else.

The meeting ended with the decision of presenting this to their parents over the weekend. In the meantime, they would send a telegram to Bill Tilison telling him they were available. If the family refused and Mr. Tilison said yes, they could always decline, or sneak out in the dark of the night.

The weekend gathering was always noisy. The food was plentiful. The three brothers would move near the workshop, enjoying cigars and a pail of beer after eating. Albert liked to sip brandy and never took up cigars. He would share in the brother's stories to the entertainment of his children. The cousins usually headed for town shortly after the meal was over, but on this weekend they sat on the porch and sipped on sweet tea. Ruth, Karen, and Jenny were busy cleaning up. The boys were kept busy running errands as needed for the ladies.

Joan and Nina noticed that the three cousins were sitting there like expectant fathers. They were fidgeting, unable to settle down, and for some unknown reason, not heading for town.

"Do you boys have something you want to talk about?" asked the observant Grandma Joan.

"Probably want to talk about the cattle drive in the paper," Albert volunteered.

They could see the cousins' faces fall in unison.

"Have you made up your minds if you're going to do it yet or not?" Karl asked.

Tony added, "We understand that you got a telegram back two days ago."

Caught flat-footed, the cousins looked at each other with true surprise on their faces. Albert had given them the paper and pointed out the ad. Their fathers did a lot of business with the telegraph office. They suddenly realized that there was no way to keep a secret in a small town. They looked up and saw that the mothers were standing at the door waiting for their answer. Grandma Joan and Grandma Nina looked on expectantly. Their fathers and Albert were staring at them, smiling from ear to ear. They were enjoying the confused look on their sons' faces.

Dan nodded. "Yup, I guess we are."

Dan felt that his answer lacked the conviction it should have had. They were all set to debate, and even beg if necessary, to be able to go. He suddenly realized that he and his cousins were being looked at as adults. Adults make their own decisions and don't ask permission. He had a twinge of regret as he felt youth slipping away.

The sudden realization that they would be leaving the homes they had known all their lives made the cousins a little somber. They answered the questions about getting a telegram from Bill Tilison offering them work. The telegram told them it would be a two-month job, starting at $30 per month. Working horses would be supplied.

Nina and Joan moved over to the glider swing and were in a serious discussion. After a bit, they nodded in agreement and settled in to watch the younger people enjoy the afternoon.

The sun was low when Dan, Vic, and Zac went to town. The lights were bright at the Grange hall. Music greeted the cousins' approach. The room was warm and filled with cigar smoke. The smell of beer and too much perfume assured them that they could look forward to a good night of dancing and drink.

Mary Schmidt spotted Dan and hurried across the dance floor to see him. Vic looked around and saw Marie with Al Blevins, the banker's son. Vic went over to the plank bar where they were serving mugs of beer. Placing a dime on the bar, Vic picked up a freshly drawn mug and blew the foam off the top.

Dan and Mary had moved to the dance floor and stepped to the music as though making up for lost time. While Mary and Marie were sisters, the two were very different. Mary was less flamboyant. She had rich brown hair that was wore in long ringlets. Her hazel eyes were always smiling. She had a trim shape that couldn't be hidden under any type of clothes. When dancing, her head came up to Dan's shoulder and often found a home there.

Marie stood flirting with Al Blevins. She was out for a good time. She had lighter brown hair and a full figure. Her green eyes always suggested she was holding something back. They were always searching the room, looking for a better opportunity.

Vic glanced at Marie and saw her look briefly at him before turning back to Al. He stepped out onto the Grange hall porch to drink his beer. As he reached for a post to lean on, Vic was bumped from the back and almost went sprawling. His beer splashed across his shirt.

Turning quickly, he stood face to face with Cal Ryan. Cal was always bigger than others his age and had realized it when he was young. He had taken a toll on most young men in the town and found pleasure in pushing people around.

"You owe me a beer, Cal," Vic said evenly.

"You're the big man in town with all that reward money. Maybe you should buy me a beer," Cal snarled.

Vic was feeling a bit sore about Marie, and the night was too warm. He wasn't in the mood to dance, so he figured that there was nothing left to do but fight. Cal stepped forward with his chest out, attempting to push Vic off the porch.

Vic grabbed the front of Cal's shirt and pulled him hard, and the two of them landed in the street raising a cloud of dust. Jumping to his feet, Vic turned toward Cal and saw Cal's ham-like fist coming at him. He turned his head just enough to turn the solid punch into a glancing blow off the corner of his eye. The blow made Vic see stars and spun him around, rolling back onto the ground.

Cal ran forward to kick Vic in the ribs. In desperation, Vic grabbed for the boot and gave it a twist and push to the side. Cal yelped as his knee was wrenched. Off balance by the push, he landed on the ground beside Vic.

Rough hands grabbed the two men and pulled them to their feet. Sheriff Wallace and his deputy pushed the two men against the porch rail.

"I would usually let you boys kill each other, but the night is hot. I don't plan to spend it dragging you scrappers to jail."

Vic's blood was boiling, and he was aching to sink his fist into Cal's belly. Cal was leaning on the rail and favoring his leg.

The sheriff continued. "Now the two of you go back in and have a beer on me. Don't make me have to talk to you again."

"You're right, sheriff," Vic agreed. "It's an awful waste of time trying to knock any sense into a skull as thick as his."

Cal growled and stepped forward, his injured knee almost making him fall. The deputy pushed him back against the rail and gave him a warning look.

"Come on, Cal. Let's have that beer on the sheriff," Vic said, trying to lighten the moment.

It was just after midnight when the three cousins returned to Vic's house looking forward to a snack they knew Grandma Joan would leave out. They were surprised to find Grandma Joan waiting on the porch.

"Getting some cool air, grandma?" Vic asked.

"The night is just starting to get comfortable," she said. "I have something on the table for you to eat, and I need to talk to you boys."

They trooped into the kitchen with Grandma Joan following them. Dan and Zac were kidding Vic about his black eye. Grandma Joan stood near the fireplace. Her face was drawn and her eyes looked tired.

Dan took a big bite of an oatmeal cookie and stopped in mid-chew when he looked at his grandmother in the lamp light. "Are you sick, grandma?"

"I haven't been sleeping lately. I have been debating whether I should tell you boys something or not. Talking with Grandma Nina today, I finally made a decision."

Joan walked over and placed a leather-bound ledger onto the table and beside it a rolled-up piece of leather tied with packaging string.

The cousins looked at the two items. They recognized the ledger. It was their Grandfather Oli's and they had seen it several times over the years. The rolled-up leather they had not seen before.

Grandma Joan untied the leather and slowly unrolled it in front of them. They recognized it as a map. But a map of what, they did not know. The leather was aged, but the markings were clear. They could see the mountains and rivers. They could see a crescent and three crosses. There were numbers and dots on the map.

Grandma Joan gazed at the map a moment before she started. "This is a treasure map. It is the map your grandfather used on his adventure. He received it from a seaman named Jolly."

"Jolly befriended your grandfather during the trip across the Atlantic from Finland to Boston. When Jolly was dying of pneumonia, he gave it to grandfather. Jolly originally got it from an old Spaniard who had gotten it handed down to him."

"Your grandfather found the gold. Some of it he brought out of the wilderness with him. Some he hid in the Black Hills. Your fathers went and found the gold he hid and brought it back to pay the note on the house."

Grandma Joan sat, looking at her grandsons. She knew the next piece of information could make their future secure, or could destroy them. This realization was what made sleeping difficult the past few nights.

The three sat silently, waiting for their grandmother to continue. "Your grandfather confided some information to me. He was not able to take all of the Spanish gold from its original hiding place. He took all he could carry and left the rest."

She watched this information slowly

sink into the grandsons' heads. They looked from one to another, with wonder on their faces.

"Are you telling us that there is more gold left in the mountains?" Dan asked.

"All I know is that there is some gold left. How much, I do not know. Between the map, notes and sketches in the ledger, you should be able to find it." She knew that what was just said could not be undone.

With the three grandsons leaning forward, the cookies forgotten, Joan pointed out the various markings on the map. She explained that the numbers were equal to days walking. The mountains were the Rockies. The main river was the Platte River. She showed them sketches and notes their grandfather had made in the ledger.

"Your grandfather knew that gold was as much of an evil as a help. The gold he carried almost killed him. Leaving the majority of it behind was the only thing that saved his life." She picked the cookies up from the table and brought them to the kitchen. Returning to the table, she continued.

"The three of you have always talked of having ranches in the West. If there is enough gold, maybe it will help your dreams come true.

"You have made a commitment to Bill Tilison of the Flying T ranch to help with the cattle drive. Once done, you will be in

Wyoming. That's the area the gold is in. You could look for it after the drive."

The three grandsons all started talking at once. Their Grandma Joan held her hand up for silence. "Now, wait. I know you will have many questions before you leave on the drive. We will have many opportunities to talk. Keep the existence of the map between yourselves. I am tired and need to sleep now." She gave each of them a hug and a kiss on the cheek, giving Zac an extra squeeze. She had always considered Zac her grandson along with the others. He was her Oli's flesh and blood.

CHAPTER FIVE

The three cousins did not get much sleep that night. After Grandma Joan went to bed, they moved out into the workshop. They set the map and ledger on the center of the workbench. They knew it made no sense to study the map and ledger right now. After a few beers and little sleep, they would no doubt miss important information.

Zac looked at his cousins. "We are still going on the drive, right?"

Dan poked at the ledger, moving it around the bench. "We told Bill Tilison we would be there. I don't think we have a choice."

"I can't believe Grandma Joan knew this all these years and did not tell our fathers," Vic said.

Zac and Dan looked at Vic. "You agree that we need to make the drive, don't you,

Vic?"

"Of course I do. Like Grandma said, 'it will take us west' and that is where the gold is," Vic said, picking up the ledger and paging through it.

Their meeting broke up around 3 a.m. and they all headed for their homes. Vic kept the map and ledger. These he put into his father Karl's safe.

The next day, two important things happened. The banker, Paul Blevins, had a brief ceremony in front of the bank presenting Dan, Vic, and Zac shares of the $1,000 reward for catching the bank robbers.

Second, a special delivery package came for the cousins from Bill Tilison. They were summoned by a very proud George Walters, who had the post office in his mercantile.

"I got a special delivery package for you boys," he announced.

"For us? Special delivery?" asked Dan. "Are you sure?"

Special delivery had been started in 1885, and it was very rare and quite expensive. To receive one was a once in a lifetime event. The package was from Bill Tilison, Kansas City, MO.

"Who would believe it? Two special delivery packages in one day," the very important-feeling postmaster and merchant bubbled.

With shaking hands, Mr. Walters handed the package to Dan and asked for a signature. The three cousins hurried out of Walter's Mercantile and headed for the workshop to open the package.

They arrived at the workshop and almost ran Karl over as he was stepping out of the door.

"Sorry, father," Vic apologized. "We got a special delivery package!"

"From who?" Karl inquired.

"It's from the Flying T," Dan offered.

With Karl watching over their shoulders, Zac took out the Good Knife and slowly slit the end of the package. It contained a letter, three train tickets, $90 cash, and a map showing the planned trail of the cattle.

The map started at Gila in the New Mexico Territory. It continued to Santa Fe and on just past Cheyenne, Wyoming.

Vic set the map aside and opened the letter.

> Gentlemen,
> I would like to thank you for agreeing to join the Flying T cattle drive. I have acquired 4,000 head of mixed breed cattle on the Gila River in New Mexico Territory. I need

to move the cattle to a ranch in Wyoming. I will also require some men to remain through the winter. If interested in remaining until next spring, let me know when you arrive.

The drive will start on July 15th. We will be in Santa Fe by the middle of August. You are to wait at the De Vargas Hotel. Included in this package are train tickets on the Atchison, Topeka and Santa Fe Railway. The cash is your first month's pay.

If you prove to be a top hand, your pay will be increased to $40 per month. At the end of your satisfactory employment, you will be provided with a ticket home or a horse. You will need to supply or purchase your own saddle.

Regards,
Bill Tilison

Each read the letter, with Karl reading it last. Zac carefully replaced the items in the package. They stood, quietly digesting the letter.

"It sounds to me like you will be working for a special kind of man," Karl said. "Sight unseen, he sends you tickets and money."

"Why do you think that is, father?" Vic asked.

"Well, my guess is he came across these cattle unexpectedly. He no doubt has vaqueros to drive them through New Mexico. They are more than likely heading back south at Santa Fe. So Bill Tilison will need more drovers. They are talking about statehood in Wyoming. He no doubt thinks there is an advantage to have a stocked ranch there."

"It makes sense to me," Dan agreed.

The Milwaukee Road train stopped in Elkader. The cousins would take this to St. Paul where they would pick up the Atchison, Topeka and Santa Fe Railway. In just over a week, they would be in Santa Fe. The fast trip from Iowa to New Mexico was almost beyond comprehension for them. The tickets had an August 4th date of departure.

The days before leaving were filled with anticipation. They were finally going west. Mary was demanding much of Dan's time. He would be gone for months. She had fallen in love and feared something would

53

happen during the trip. Vic and Zac had no romantic ties and their only worry was selecting the proper western clothes.

There were three stacks containing items needed for the trip. Each contained a saddle, saddlebags, canteen, lariat rope, pigging strings, spare clothes, ground cover and blanket, rain slicker, Colt .44 and holster, Winchester rifles, saddle scabbards, mess kits, toiletry items, odds and ends for repairing and fixing things. Food would be added by their mothers just before leaving. Chaps would be purchased in Santa Fe.

The three sat in the workshop going over and over the list of items.

"Can you think of anything else we are overlooking?" Vic asked, his brow furled with concern.

"Vic, we have been over the list a dozen times. We have too much weight for the cattle drive already. If anything, we should cut back items," Zac urged.

Dan was busy putting his belongings together for travel. He wanted to spend time with Mary this evening. "You guys can spend the whole evening debating, but I have someone to see before we leave."

Finishing, Dan left the workshop and headed home to see his folks before going to meet Mary for supper.

Vic and Zac stared at his packs. He did a fine job of putting everything in its place and having a place for everything. They looked at the piles of items they had to stow.

"Damn fine packing Dan did. We best get started, Zac, if we plan to be done before morning."

Supper at the Elkader Café had been quiet. Dan and Mary purposely avoided the subject of his leaving. Each of them knew that after tomorrow it would be a long time before they were together again. Dan held the door as Mary stepped out of the café. Going straight home was out of the question.

The August evening was cool and Mary pulled her wrap a bit tighter. The clear night sky was filled with stars. She and Dan walked near the recently completed Keystone Bridge. They leaned over the stone wall, looking at the Turkey River.

Mary pressed close to Dan. She had decided Dan was hers when they were still in grade school.

"Remember, Dan, when you get your ranch out west, I will be ready to join you."

"It will be the first thing I do. I promise." He kissed her lightly on the cheek.

Mary wrapped her arms around him and buried her face in his chest to hide the tears that were welling in her eyes.

* * *

The train arrived at the Elkader

station, belching smoke and steam as it rolled to a stop. The family and friends had come to wish the cousins farewell and a safe journey. Karl brought a small pack with him.

"Not more food, I hope. Mother has given us more than we will be able to eat already," Vic joked.

"I'm not sure you guys could be given enough food," Karl laughed. "No, this is something every traveler to the West needs."

Reaching into the pack, he removed three small boxes with their grandfather's fire starter. Smiling, the boys took the boxes and tucked them in their saddlebags. Karl then held up his sheepskin vest.

"Vic, I haven't worn this in years. Where you're going, you may need it." He slipped the vest onto his son. Vic went to button it and felt something heavy in the pocket. Slipping his hand into the pocket, he felt a derringer.

"Don't let people know you have it," he cautioned. "It's a sneak gun."

Dan and Mary stood off to the side. Dan remembered the feel of her tears on his shirt. Today, she held up a good front. Smiling and chatting, she held his hand.

"Now, you remember to write me, Dan August," Mary said, with a firm look on her face.

Zac was talking with his father when he suddenly stopped. There stood Cal Ryan with his brother Wally at the far end of the platform. Both were dragging saddles and bags containing their other items. They slung their holsters and guns over their shoulders. The two were disheveled and apparently had spent the previous night out on the town.

Cal saw the August cousins. "You boys going somewhere?" he sneered.

"We have a job on a cattle drive," Zac replied. He could feel the hair prickling on the back of his neck.

Cal turned to Wally. "Suppose we will have to babysit these boys the rest of the summer."

Vic, Dan, and Zac watched the Ryans get on the train. Zac stood clenching and unclenching his fists. He knew that a time would come when they would have to put them into their place?

Tony saw the exchange of looks between the Ryans and their sons. He decided to break up the tension, "Let's grab this stuff and get you on the train. You don't want to get left standing on the platform."

Grabbing their gear, the cousins climbed into the passenger car.

"Put the saddle in the boxcar ahead," a good-looking cowboy said, "and stow the rest of your stuff overhead, or under your seats."

"Thanks, friend," Dan said as they stowed their gear. He wondered if he could ever look as much of a cowboy as that fellow.

Settled in, they felt the train lurch as it pulled out of the station. The cousins waved to the family and friends. Soon, their view was obscured by clouds of black smoke. The opposite window gave them a view of the buildings of Elkader moving past: The sawmill with large mounds of sawdust; the gristmill with flour dust blowing out the vents; empty rail cars on the spur waiting to be filled with goods. All were left behind as the train gathered speed.

Dan wondered how long it would be before they got back home. After the cattle drive, and if they found the gold, they would be starting up ranches. It could be years before any of them saw Elkader again. Would he ever see their grandmothers again? The excitement of getting on the train began to wane and it was replaced with a heavy feeling in the pit of his stomach.

The sound of Cal and Wally cutting up further back in the car could be heard. Glancing, Dan noticed they were passing a bottle. Vic had his saddlebag open and was digging into his food. He brought out a large piece of cornbread. Zac was staring out of the window, deep in his own thoughts.

The train car was old and the seats uncomfortable. They were of the bench design, stuffed with horse hair. The leather covers were well-worn and stained by past passengers. The farmland was moving by. It was late afternoon and Vic pointed to some young farm boys chasing the cows toward the barn for milking. A yellow and brown dog ran from side to side, keeping the cows moving. The boys waved at the train.

"That's what we will be doing in a couple of weeks," Vic smiled. "I am damn glad we won't have to milk those 4,000 cows."

The train wheels clacked on each seam of the rails, setting up a constant rhythmic noise. Zac sat quietly, wondering if he would be able to sleep with the noise. The train pulled into a small town around supper time. The brakeman shouted out that their stop would be 30 minutes and food was available at the Railside Café.

People tumbled out of the train cars, hurrying to the café. The café had dingy-looking curtains and tables with chipped white paint. The plank floor had a well-worn path from the doorway to the counter.

The cousins stood in line, watching a heavy-set lady with dirty gray hair in a loose bun and wearing a stained apron, handing out paper packages containing two thick ham sandwiches. Beside her was a pretty redheaded girl offering cool bottles of some type of pop. She had freckles across her nose and emerald, green eyes that twinkled.

Vic noticed a family resemblance between the cute redhead and the dirty gray-haired lady. He smiled at the girl when she handed him the pop, but shuddered inside, thinking what would happen to her in future years.

A tired-looking white-haired man in a dirty gray shirt and suspenders was taking money at the end of the counter. He was charging thirty-five cents for the sandwiches and pop. There was a worn cigar box in front of him where he kept change.

The café had a sour smell and the cousins were glad to get back to the coal smell of the train. They sat back in their seats. Zac noticed that his saddlebags had been moved. A quick check confirmed that nothing was gone. He decided that in the future one of them would stay on the train to guard their gear.

The sandwiches were surprisingly good. The coarse ground flour used to make the bread made chewing a bit more work, but the ham was sliced thick and had a good flavor. Dan removed the wire cap from the bottle of pop. Taking a sip, he smiled. "Root beer, my favorite."

A bit late, the train continued out of the country station with its normal amount of lurching and sounds of steel spinning on steel. They would be in St. Paul very early the next morning. It would be a full day before they caught the Atchison, Topeka and Santa Fe Train. A branch line was required to get to the main line.

Vic finished his second sandwich and washed it down with the last of his pop. Getting up, he headed for the toilet in the back of the car. The wooden door was scarred and rattled on its hinges. Vic stepped in and the strong smell of urine hit his nostrils. With the swaying and bumping of the train, many a man may have had trouble with his aim. He looked down in the toilet hole and could see the railroad ties flashing by.

Happy to be back in the stale air of the railroad car, Vic slowly moved toward his seat. He made every attempt not to bump into any of the sleeping passengers. He noticed Cal and Wally draped over two seats. They were snoring loudly in their drunken stupor. He had seen them running for the Rail Side Tavern when they'd stopped for supper.

Zac and Dan were sleeping. Vic hoped he would fall asleep soon to close the railcar world out. Using his saddlebags for a pillow, he curled up on the seat and was soon sleeping.

The blast of the steam whistle and skidding of wheels against the rails shook the sleepy passengers awake. Dan looked out at the darkened buildings. It would be another two hours before the sun came up. As the train stopped and the doors opened, the cousins grabbed their gear and stiffly stepped out onto the platform.

Piling their gear on the edge of the

platform, the cousins watched the activity of goods being unloaded and passengers slowly wandering away. Soon the train sat quietly and the platform was vacant. Leaning against the station wall, they dozed off and on.

"You boys interested in some coffee?" They looked up at the whisker-covered chin of an old codger. When he smiled, they could see his stained yellow teeth in the lantern light.

"You bet we would," Vic answered without hesitation.

The bent old man led them into a side door of the station and grabbed three tin cups. Handing them to the cousins, he pointed to the coffee pot on the potbelly stove.

"I come in early to make coffee for the morning crews. Help yourselves, and drag your gear in here so it don't walk away."

The coffee was strong and the room was warm. The old codger went into the next room and soon they smelled bacon frying. Their stomachs began to growl. Zac was just about to dig into his food pack when the oldster stepped back in the room holding a blackened three prong fork.

"Bacon's on. Got enough for the three of you you are hungry."

The three cousins tripped over each other running toward the delicious smell. They were treated to biscuits and bacon. He even gave them each two cold boiled eggs.

They washed it all down with more hot, strong coffee.

"You going into town?"

"We need to waste the day. We thought we would take in the sights," Dan volunteered.

"I recommend you see the upper and lower landings. Lots of stuff going on there. We got us a cable car. Goes right along, no horses needed. You should ride that. A good place to eat is the Ryan Hotel. I would be glad to keep your gear here until train time. If I'm not here, Carlos will be."

"Why, thank you. By the way, my name is Dan. These other two are Vic and Zac. We are the August cousins."

"These old bones are called Huck. Yes sir, you stay to the main streets and you'll not have any trouble." Huck hobbled over to the basin and set his fry pan in it.

"You want us to help you clean up here?" Zac asked.

Huck waved them away. "Not necessary. I don't have much to do. This keeps me busy."

The cousins stepped out into the early morning sun and looked toward the Mississippi River. They spent the morning walking around the lower landing and looking at the brightly colored steamboats. As they moved away from the landing, great clouds of black smoke billowed out of their stacks. The water swirled behind them from the side wheels.

There was talk of a showboat coming up from New Orleans, bringing a Shakespeare play into the area. There was still talk about the steamboat Natchez VIII that burnt earlier that year in Lake Providence, Louisiana.

Vic asked for directions to the closest location of the new cable car. They stepped onto the car and sat on the stiff, straight back benches. There was a cable running in the groove between the tracks. It appeared to be attached to the car by some method underneath the car. The conductor told them that it was connected with a "grip".

They rode the car up East 7th Street. Zac held on to the back of the seat in front of him, his knuckles white. His jaw was set and his eyes looked straight ahead.

Vic poked Dan in the ribs. "I think Zac is ready to jump any time," he whispered.

The cable car stopped. Zac hurried off and grabbed the light pole on the side of the street to steady himself.

"There was nothing in front to stop us. It felt like we were rolling out of control," Zac grumbled.

Vic and Dan laughed, then headed a block over to the Ryan Hotel. Zac watched the car depart before he followed them. The plan was to have a nice meal and then return to the train station.

It was starting to get dark as they headed back to the station. The huge warehouses deepened the shadows even more. Vic spoke in a hushed voice, "We got four guys pacing us next to the buildings."

"I have been watching them for a while," Zac answered in a low voice.

They approached some stacked boxes of freight and when they emerged on the other side, two of the men had disappeared. Dan glanced around carefully, trying to spot them. As they passed some stacks of barbed wire, Zac ducked out of sight. Dan and Vic continued to walk, chatting aimlessly, but watching the remaining two men.

Suddenly, the two turned to a route that would cross theirs. Slightly ahead of Vic and Dan, they stopped and turned. They held short clubs in their hands.

The bigger, husky thug slapped the short club in his other hand. "We saw you spending freely in the Ryan Hotel. We figure you should give us what you have left."

Dan and Vic moved slightly apart. "We will ask you once, and only once, to move and give us the right of way," Vic warned.

Snorting, the shorter of the two thugs raised his club. "Kind of cocky, aren't you? I guess we will have to teach you young pups."

"If you are expecting help from your two confederates behind us, they won't be coming," Dan said casually. "In fact, they just might need your help."

The two thugs shifted uneasily for a moment. Then looking at the two in front of them, they regained their courage. With raised clubs they stepped forward.

"I would stop!" Vic snapped, "unless you desire to die tonight. We are carrying weapons far more deadly than your clubs. One more step and you will both be clutching knives in your chests."

"And if necessary, I will send one into one of your throats." It was Zac behind them.

Realizing that the plan was foiled, the two thugs ran between the buildings and disappeared into the darkness.

"You didn't hurt the others too much, did you?" Vic asked.

"They will have about a two-day headache. My club was bigger than theirs," Zac chuckled.

Carlos had the coffee on when the cousins got back. "Huck told me to watch your gear. The train doesn't leave for another hour. Grab a seat and have some coffee."

Carlos was younger-looking than Huck. He had thick, bushy eyebrows and shaggy salt and pepper hair that had not seen a comb in some time. His broad shoulders were evidence of hard work in the past.

Sitting next to the potbelly stove, Carlos got the tip of a long cigar glowing.

"Huck and I helped build these railroads. We didn't earn too much, but it was steady work. Huck had a stack of ties collapse on him. It busted his legs up a bit. We left the railroad building business and have worked here ever since."

The sound of a couple of drunks stumbling by made the group turn and look. It was Cal and Wally. They had made poor use of their time in St. Paul.

Carlos shook his head. "More than likely visited the working ladies. Whatever money they had, they will find missing in the morning."

CHAPTER SIX

The Atchison, Topeka and Santa Fe Train was more comfortable than the Milwaukee. The good-looking cowboy was still riding with them. Cal and Wally were ill-tempered after their visit to St. Paul, but thankfully kept to themselves. Dan had seen them selling some items from their bags to other passengers. They needed the money to eat during the 1200-mile trip to Santa Fe.

The cousins watched with avid interest as the landscape turned from rolling grassy plains to a more arid land with mesquite and greasewood. When they saw their first cactus, with its arms reaching out, they were struck speechless. They traveled through valleys with steep sandstone walls. Large boulders were scattered across the valley floors.

The conductor told them that the train actually stopped in Lamy, New Mexico which was about 14 miles south of Santa Fe. When the tracks were being laid, it was more practical to go that way rather than through Santa Fe. There was a mercantile and saloon in Lamy where they could get a meal. A wagon would take them to the De Vargas hotel in Santa Fe.

Lamy was hot and dry. The cousins picked up their gear and walked from the train station to the mercantile to wait for the wagon. Their breathing was heavy as they got to the mercantile. Dan complained about a headache.

"It's the high altitude," the good-looking cowboy informed them. "You are over 6,000 feet. Santa Fe is even higher, over 7,000 feet."

Extending his hand to the cousins, he shook them all around. "Don't worry, give yourself a little time and you will get used to the altitude. My name is Rod Tilison. We are here to drive my father's cattle."

Rod was of average height and above-average looks. He had neatly-combed brown hair and hazel eyes. He had a fair complexion and a firm jaw with a dimple in the end of his chin. His Colt revolver was low on his hip and tied down. The clothes were tailored to fit his lean body.

The cousins watched him walk into the

mercantile to make arrangements for the wagon. Cal and Wally sat heavily not far from them. They were complaining about the heat and looked like they might have lost a few pounds during the week trip down from St. Paul.

Rod Tilison stepped out of the mercantile. "The wagon will be here in an hour. In the meantime, the chow is on me in the saloon."

He then added, "No beer or whiskey."

The Ryan brothers ate like they had been without a good meal in some time. There was a spread of meat and cheese with thick slices of bread. A large pot of hot coffee and a bucket of cool well water were available for the thirsty crew.

Dan, Vic, and Zac ate two thick sandwiches each and washed it down with cool well water. Rod smiled at the cousins.

"I see the altitude sickness is getting better. Well, eat up. We have a five-hour wagon ride ahead of us. We won't get to Santa Fe until after dark."

Finishing up, the cousins went to the mercantile and looked for items they might have overlooked. They each bought a pair of chaps and a couple of extra neckerchiefs. Three boxes of .44 shells rounded out their purchases. While settling up with the clerk, they heard the wagons pulling up.

One of the wagons was filled with

supplies and the other would carry a total of eight men, including Rod Tilison. With their gear stowed on the second wagon, the men began to climb on. Rod climbed into the seat and picked up the reins. He motioned Dan to sit with him.

It was mid-afternoon when the wagons rolled out. The day was still and hot. Their clothes stuck to their sweating bodies. The horses' hooves created wisps of dust as they pulled the loaded wagons. Lamy slowly disappeared from sight.

The surrounding countryside looked like something out of another world. In the distance they could see mountains shaded in brown and purple. Their peaks etched the skyline. Nearby were hills covered with aspen or scrubby evergreens. The valley floor was a mixture of cactus and twisted shrubs. Splashes of color could be seen from flowers struggling to survive in the arid climate. The dominant look was shades of brown.

Having lived in grass-covered areas all their lives, it was difficult to understand what the cattle could eat in this country. What they did not realize was that many of the succulent plants made very good feed for cattle. The land could not support the density that grasslands could.

They passed an occasional cluster of adobe buildings. Young, black-haired children stood and watched the slow-moving wagons. The women bent over their cook fires, making tortillas to wrap around a combination of meat, vegetables, peppers, or beans for their evening meal. A bell rang off in the distance. It was probably from a small church calling parishioners to Mass.

After two hours, Rod stopped the wagons in the shade of a tilted rock ledge to give the horses a breather. He cautioned everyone about rattlesnakes before they climbed down to relieve themselves.

Rod and Dan took turns driving the wagon. Vic watched as Rod pointed out various things along the trail. Zac appeared to be dozing, but Vic knew that he was watching and memorizing landmarks. With their bellies full, Cal and Wally lay curled up in the back of the wagon sleeping. There were two Texans, Jack and Abe, who had joined them in Lamy.

Jack Walls was lean, and had a large nose matched by his big ears. Abe Shute was tall, with a bit of a stoop of his shoulders. He had a long face and spoke slowly and distinctly. He had gotten the nickname Abe because it was said that he looked like Lincoln. Both had bowed legs from hanging onto a horse. Their well-worn holsters were filled with well-oiled guns. There was no doubt the two were top hands and were already getting paid $40 a month.

It was after dark when the wagons

pulled in front of the De Vargas Hotel. The brick and wood building with tall windows facing the street was lit up and a welcome sight. The air was quickly becoming cooler after the sun went down. The warm glow of the hotel looked very inviting.

"We have an early morning trip to the herd tomorrow," Rod instructed. "Grab only what you need for the night from the wagon, leave the rest. Your gear will be watched."

Vic ran his hand along the heavy wooden trim that decorated the lobby. It reminded him of some of the work his father had done.

All of the riders were tired, and after a quick supper in the hotel dining room they straggled up to the rooms. Vic, Dan, and Zac shared the same room. Cal, Wally and the two Texans shared another. The bathroom was down the hall.

The metal springs creaked under the soft mattress as the cousins settled in. It barely felt like they had closed their eyes when there came a wake-up knock on the door. Tumbling out of the beds, they trooped down to the bathroom and cleaned up before heading for breakfast. Dan mentioned that this would be the last time that they would sleep in a bed for the next couple of months. The hotel had running water from a tank on the roof. They took full advantage of it washing up.

The dining room was set for breakfast. There were smells of bread baking for use later in the day. Breakfast was served boarding house-style, with dishes of scrambled eggs and platters of bacon. There was thick-sliced bread to be slathered with butter. A bowl of jam sat next to the bread. Hot coffee was poured by a young Mexican boy in a stiff white shirt.

Vic, Dan, and Zac sat at a table near the window so they could watch the sun come up. Rod pulled up a chair and joined them.

He waved his arm around the room. "This is much fancier than I would have liked, but it was this or one of the south town hotels, which are nothing more than large rooms with lice ridden bunks."

"How far is the herd?" Vic asked.

"It's about five miles east of here. There is water, but not much grazing. A herd the size of ours needs a lot of feed. That's why we have to get there early. We will be picking up the herd while it is moving." Rod scooped some eggs onto his plate. "The wrangler has some horses waiting for us. We should reach the herd around midday and will relieve some of the men."

They gave their full attention to devouring the food in front of them. With their plates clean, they leaned back to enjoy some more coffee.

"I've been watching you three coming

down here.   You know how to handle yourselves and appear to be men that can be trusted to do the job assigned."

Rod set his coffee cup down. "My father bought this herd, fair and square. Some of the cows he bought may not have been gotten as fairly."

"The herd is being followed by men that would like to take some of the cattle back south.   There was a quick encounter with them on the Gila River. I would like you three to work as scouts, riding ahead and to the sides of the herd.

"My father read about your capturing the Alan gang after you accepted the drive. He recommended you be offered the jobs. The pay is higher, $40 a month. You will still be working with the cattle on occasion, but your main job is to be the eyes and ears of the herd."

The three sat staring at Rod as he spoke, their coffee getting cold. His offer had come out of the blue.   They had never considered themselves as scout material.

"We would be happy to accept your offer," Vic was quick to reply.

Riding away from the herd meant eating less dust. They would be watching for trouble and would be putting themselves in danger.   They realized that there was also danger around the herd.   A man could be gored by a steer, trampled in a stampede, or thrown by a horse's misstep, pushing an animal back into the herd.

After breakfast, the three walked out onto the hotel walk. Dan took out the makings and began to roll a smoke. He had picked up the habit while traveling on the train. He had smoked a cigar on occasion back home. Lighting a match with his thumbnail, he lit the cigarette and took a long drag.

"Smoking them things could be the death of a man," Vic warned. "A bad man can smell the smoke or see the glow from a long way and get a shot at you before you know he is around."

Zac walked to the wagon and checked their gear. All appeared as they had left it. Vic and Dan joined him. They got their guns from their saddlebags and strapped them on. With their new assignment and Rod's warnings, they decided they'd best be ready for whatever came.

CHAPTER SEVEN

Rod walked toward the wagon, followed by a grizzled old stable hand leading three horses. There was a chestnut with white markings, a bay, and a black and white piebald. The horses all had long legs, and according to the stable hand, were mountain-bred.

"I got these horses for you after you agreed to scout. I figured it would be best if you rode to the herd. It will give you a better lay of the land. Leave your bedrolls, saddlebags, and chaps in the wagon."

The cousins got busy saddling the horses. The Ryans scowled and looked on. The two Texans were indifferent and leaned against the wagon. Dan took the chestnut, Vic the bay, and Zac the piebald. The horses were all geldings. They held their heads high and were alert to all movements around them. Zac smiled, realizing that they had been given some very fine horse flesh.

Vic looked up at the sound of a galloping horse. What he saw stopped him cold. On a buckskin mare sat a young blond girl. Her hat had blown off her head and hung on her back. Her blouse was of Spanish design, and she had a split skirt and rode astride the horse. Her cheeks were flushed from the cool morning air, and her eyes had a mischievous smile.

Rod waved to her. "Good morning, sis. Glad to see I don't have to go looking for you."

He turned to introduce them. "This is my sister, Carla. She will be traveling with us to Wyoming."

Dan noticed the two Texans shaking their heads. It was obvious that they did not like the idea of a woman on the drive.

Vic nudged Dan. "The Texans might not like having Carla on the drive, but I sure do."

"Best pull in your horns, Vic," Dan cautioned. "Remember, she is the owner's daughter and the boss' sister."

With their mounts saddled and ready to go, Dan walked up to Rod.

"Is there anything special you would like us to check out today?"

"My sister doesn't want to stay with the wagons. If one of you could escort her to the herd, I would appreciate it. Other than that, just get familiar with the territory and make sure nobody is following too close." Rod turned away quickly when the teamster on the other wagon called to him.

Vic swung onto his horse. It felt great to be back in his saddle. He had grabbed his vest to ward off the morning chill. He could feel the cold derringer in the pocket. He turned his horse toward Dan and Zac.

"I heard the instructions, Dan. I think I should escort Carla to the herd," Vic said with conviction.

Laughing, Dan looked at Zac. "It is always nice to have a volunteer, isn't it, Zac?"

Looking at his older cousin, Zac teased, "Just don't let her lose you on the way,"

Carla walked out of the hotel with a thick piece of bread with butter and jam in her hand. Vic rode up to her. "I will be joining you on the ride to the herd. By the way, my name is Vic August."

Carla gave him a scrutinizing look as she wiped a bit of jam off the corner of her mouth. Flipping her hair, she said, "My brother must have been afraid you couldn't find the herd. Very well, just follow me."

Vic's first impulse was to correct her on who was leading who, but decided it was better to observe the object of his interest before he burnt a bridge that couldn't be rebuilt.

Finishing her bread, Carla put on her flat-brimmed hat and her riding gloves. With little effort, she swung into the saddle and spurred her horse into action. Vic, caught by surprise, was left several lengths behind her.

Dan and Zac watched them gallop away from the group, leaving behind a trail of dust.

Rod had told them that the herd should be directly east of Santa Fe. It would only be traveling about 12 miles a day. The route they were taking to Colorado was between the Rio Grande and Pecos Rivers. Much of it was high desert. Water and grazing would be fair at best. The plan was to find and follow the most favorable route.

There was a ramrod who had taken cattle north to Denver before. He had suggested the San Luis Valley. Rod planned to depend heavily on his recommendations. It was late in the year to drive a herd. The spring rains were long gone, and along with it many of the succulent grasses.

Dan turned his horse and started out with a plan to intersect south of the herd's trail. Zac rode up alongside Dan. Dan noticed that while Zac had the Good Knife in the nape of his neck, he also had a second knife in his boot.

The morning sun was low in the sky and made seeing any distance difficult. Vic and Carla had disappeared behind a ridge and were walking their horses. Maybe Carla didn't want to get to the herd too fast, Dan thought.

Birds were singing their morning songs. Some bluejays scolded them as they rode by. Dan and Zac decided to separate about a half mile to cover more ground. They were concentrating on tracks left by any groups of riders.

Dan noticed a small farm with sagging corrals and two adobe buildings. The larger of the two buildings served as the barn. A short Mexican with a large straw sombrero was bringing water up from a hand-dug well.

"Mind if I water my horse?" Dan inquired.

The elderly man looked up and smiled broadly with strong white teeth. "Help yourself. There is a trough next to the barn. I got a nice cold bucket here for you."

The chestnut drank sparingly from the trough. Dan took a long drink from the dipper offered by the man.

"My name is Andre Santos. Welcome to my humble farm."

"That is mighty fine water, Andre," Dan replied. "My name is Dan August. It is a pleasure to make your acquaintance."

Dan looked around at the scrawny cattle grazing below them in the valley. There were several goats playing in the sun near the barn. Looking back toward the house, he saw an elderly woman walking toward them with a fired clay platter. On it she had soft cheese, peppers, and tortillas.

It was barely midday and Dan was not hungry. Not wanting to refuse their hospitality, Dan wrapped some peppers and cheese in a tortilla.

"My wife Rose makes the cheese from the goats' milk. She never lets a stranger leave with an empty belly," Andre said proudly.

Dan soon realized that Rose spoke no English. She set the platter down on a wooden bench near the barn. She smiled a toothless smile and walked back to the house.

Dan took a large bite of the tortilla. After a couple of chews, he felt the heat spread through his mouth. He chewed and swallowed quickly, not daring to breathe. It was his first experience with jalapeños. Taking the dipper, he took a drink of the water. It did nothing to cool his mouth.

Seeing his distress, Andre spoke quickly. "I should have warned you about the peppers. Jalapeños can be a bit rough on the tongue." He brought some goats' milk up from the well and filled a clay mug for Dan.

Dan drank the rich creamy milk and it helped marginally. Dan picked the rest of the peppers off his tortilla before taking the next bite. The cheese had a sharp but desirable flavor. Surprised at how hungry he actually was, Dan ate a second and washed it down with the rest of the milk.

Sitting on the edge of the water trough, Dan asked Andre, "Have you seen any groups of riders in the last day or two?"

"I have not seen groups. When the herd was passing the farm east of here, there were two men watching it. They came to the farm after and watered their horses. They reminded me of the Comancheros of the past. They carry rifles and many bullets. One had gold in his front teeth. The other had a long knife scar across the right side of his face."

"They stayed only a short time, and left after eating some food and using my water. We have had no trouble in this area since the Comanches were beaten in 1875. Seeing these men brought back bad memories."

After spending a few more minutes with the old gentleman, Dan climbed back onto his horse. He waved to Andre and his wife, Rose, who came to the door to watch him leave. It was now high noon and the sun was hot on Dan's back.

* * *

Zac continued riding south of Dan. He noticed a gnarled pine leaning from an outcrop of rock. It would offer some shade, so he pulled his horse over to the tree and dismounted. He was surprised to find remnants of a recent fire. An empty tequila bottle was broken against the rock, another lay on the ground nearby. Several cheroot butts lay next to the fire.

He tied his horse to a pine branch and then slowly canvassed the area. He determined that two men had been here for some time within the past couple of days. Based on boot prints and indentions left by hands and elbows, they had been watching something east of their location.

Zac found where they had tied up their horses. Nearby there was a trickle of water coming from the rock ledge, and it collected in a small pool. He drank first and then let his horse drink.

There was grass below the pool. Zac picketed the piebald on the grass and then went back to the pine tree to eat a cold meal. He watched the valley in front of him. Chewing on the biscuit and cold roast beef, he could just make out what might be the trail of the herd below.

It was mid-morning when Vic and Carla rode up to the edge of a long valley. Below them was the cattle drive. Vic was genuinely impressed. The 4,000 cattle were strung out over a mile. A long, low cloud of dust drifted with the breeze to the east. He could see the chuck wagon about a half mile in front of the herd.

"I'll go catch up with Ling in the chuck

wagon. You better check with the ramrod," Carla advised.

Vic figured his job of delivering her safely to the herd was done. She had spent the whole ride keeping him in his place. Right now, he was a bundle of mixed emotions. Vic rode in the direction of the herd and Carla galloped her horse toward the chuck wagon.

She waved to the small Asian driving the team. Ling had been with the Tilison family for as long as Carla could remember. He had driven the chuck wagon for every drive that was made when the Flying T was located in Texas.

The cattle were brought up the Chisholm Trail and later the Western Trail. She often rode on the chuck wagon with Ling during the later drives.

"Hello, Miss Tilison. I see you have found us," Ling yelled.

"I missed your burnt steaks and crunchy beans. I would travel miles for one of your memorable meals," she shouted back.

Vic rode the bay toward the herd and headed for the cowboy riding flank.

"My name's Vic August. I brought Miss Tilison here. Now I got to find the ramrod. Can you point the way?" he asked.

The dust-covered cowboy looked him over. "I'm Kelly. Eddie, our ramrod, just headed back to check on the drag."

"Thanks." Wheeling the bay, he trotted

to find the ramrod.

He saw a stocky Mexican with a wide sombrero and lots of silver on his saddle. He had an old Army Colt on his left hip and a large Bowie Knife on his right. On his saddle he carried a leather riata and a coiled whip. Eddie turned as Vic rode toward him.

"You're one of the new men from Santa Fe?"

"That I am. My name is Vic August. Mr. Tilison asked me to bring his sister to the herd," Vic said.

"I am Eduardo Garcia. They call me Eddie." He flashed a wide smile. "Get yourself a fresh horse from the remuda and ride with Kelly on the flank."

It was late afternoon when Zac caught up with Dan. The herd was an hour ahead of them and they could still taste the dust hanging in the air.

"I found a spot where men were watching the herd," Zac said. "It looked like the tracks of two men."

"You said there were two of them?" Dan asked. "I have been cutting the tracks of two riders all afternoon. I met an old Mexican who thinks he saw them. One has gold in his front teeth and the other has a scar on his right cheek.

"He said they remind him of the Comancheros. I saw fear in his eyes as he recalled them. Cousin, I think we have our work cut out for us."

They caught up to the herd at sunset. The drovers had just finished settling the herd down and were riding toward the chuck wagon. Dan estimated the crew was made up of 20 men, including the ones left with the herd.

They spotted Vic riding in. That is, they identified him by the way he sat his horse. Other than that, the dust covered man was unrecognizable.

"Hey Vic, did you get Miss Carla here alright?" Dan called.

Vic turned, brushing the dust from his clothes with his hat. "I not only got her here safely, but I also got a good taste of driving cattle."

There was the sound of a spoon banging a pan. It was a small Chinaman calling the crew to supper.

"That's our cook, Ling. I had some of his biscuits this afternoon. They were mighty good," Vic informed them.

Rod was talking to Eddie when they rode in. He waved them over.

"Eddie, these are the men I was telling you about. They will be ranging around the herd watching for any of the riffraff we ran into on the Gila."

Introductions were made around, and then Dan and Vic brought them up to date with what they had found.

"The one with the gold teeth calls himself Juan. The other sounds like Filipe," Eddie believed. "These men run with a gang of cutthroats terrorizing folks along the border. Must be they are making claim to some of our cows."

Rod nodded. "I have heard about Juan. It is unlike him to work this far north for a few cows. I figure someone hired men to bring the whole herd back. That would mean there are an awful lot of them."

He gave a worried glance toward his sister, who was kidding with Ling.

Dan looked the other cowboys over. They all had six guns and had the look that said they knew how to use them. Rod had chosen a fighting crew. That gave him some comfort.

Rod thanked Dan and Zac for the information and told them to get some chow. The beef steaks and beans were very good. A pot of coffee you could stand a poker in sat next to the fire. It was perfect for cutting the day's dust.

Cal and Wally sat near the fire, covered with dust and eating their third helping of beans. Cal glared at Dan and Zac when they came to fill their cups with coffee.

"You dandies spend your day lying under a shade tree?" Cal sneered.

"Our job is to make sure you don't get your butt shot off," Zac advised.

Dan and Vic were setting up their bedrolls when they heard some commotion near the fire. Zac had just gone back to get some more coffee. Dan and Vic walked over to see what was going on.

Two lanky drovers had Zac trapped next to the chuck wagon. Cal and Wally stood nearby, smiling evil grins.

"We don't cotton to back-shootin' Injuns," the taller one with narrow eyes was saying. "We kill 'em back home and leave 'em for the coyotes to eat."

The Ryan brothers joined in laughing with the lanky drovers.

Vic felt anger race through his body. He moved to step into the fracas, but Dan stopped him. They stood in the shadows, watching.

Zac looked at the two drovers. "You will be pleased to know you won't have to worry about being back shot. In just about a second, I am going to put a knife in the center of each of your chests. Then as you're laying on the ground begging and pleading for life, I am going to empty the coffee pot you're keeping me from down your gurgling throats. I refuse to see any man die without one last cup of coffee."

Pausing a moment, Zac continued. "By the way, if you think I can't do it, just ask the two hoot owls standing next to you."

The two drovers stepped back a bit,

suddenly uncertain of the cold-eyed man in front of them. They looked over and saw Cal and Wally heading for their bed rolls.

Weakly, the shorter one said, "We was just kidding you, with it being your first day on the drive. Hope you don't take offence."

They followed the Ryan's toward the bedrolls. Dan and Vic heard them muttering to each other as they went. As Dan and Vic turned to go back, they noticed Eddie standing in the dark. He had his whip in his left hand.

"Your friend has a lot of sand. He would do to ride the river with," Eddie said and then turned toward his bedroll.

The camp noise disappeared, with the exception of sporadic snoring. The bawling of cattle came from the herd, along with the soft out-of-tune singing of the cowboys on watch. The hills came alive with the sounds of coyotes, owls, and crickets. Vic, Dan, and Zac were soon asleep.

CHAPTER EIGHT

The eastern sky was just light when Vic woke up. He saw that the fire had already been built, and Ling was standing at the back of the chuck wagon kneading biscuits. He had a pot of water boiling over the fire for making grits. The coffee pot was next to the fire, and the smell of the strong brew made getting up much easier.

Vic saw Carla next to the chuck wagon. She was brushing out her shoulder-length blond hair. He noticed she was wearing men's trousers. She tied her hair into a bun on top of her head and then carefully put her hat over it.

Her intentions became clear to Vic. She was attempting to look like one of the men. It would only give someone following them more incentive if they knew there was a young woman with the drive.

Along with the snakes, the cousins were warned about spiders, scorpions, and other biting things getting in their boots. Vic carefully shook his out before pulling them on. Just as he headed for the coffee, he heard Dan and Zac start moving behind him.

Vic, Dan, and Zac sat to one side, enjoying large bowls of grits with gravy. How Ling came up with gravy they did not know. Men were moving around, taking care of morning duties and getting ready for the day's drive. The bedrolls and other extra gear were carried in a second wagon known as the "hoodlum". It was driven by an old Mexican called Pep.

Dan and Zac could tell that Vic had something on his mind. "There is a chance that something could happen to any one of us on this drive. I think we each need a copy of the map just in case."

He had the ledger and the rolled-up map lying on the ground next to him. He removed two pages from the back of the ledger. Each was a duplicate of the map and its markings. He handed one to Dan and one to Zac.

"Keep them in a safe place. I just figure if we are prepared, we will never need them." Vic slipped the ledger back into his saddlebag.

The three sat, drinking their coffee. The conversation changed over to scouting for the herd. Eddie had confirmed that they were being followed by dangerous men. The cousins suddenly felt the weight of their responsibility to prevent a surprise attack on the cattle drive.

A scout was on point and they knew what that was. Stories had been told about soldiers on point and their chances of surviving when Dan's father, Karl, reminisced about the War Between the States.

The next three days were hot and sunny. There was very little wind, so the dust hung heavily over the herd. Eddie let them stretch the line of cows out and stagger them to help with the dust.

Vic, Dan, and Zac rode off from the herd, looking for any sign of riders. Each day they would find the tracks of two riders. The riders were good at keeping out of sight, but their tracks were recognizable to the cousins.

They would rotate their position. One would ride out ahead, covering an area of about 15 miles. The other two would ride to the sides and back, about half a day's drive. They would then join up and ride back to the herd.

On the fourth day, Zac cut the tracks of four riders coming up from the south. The four were staying well west of the cattle trail. None of the tracks matched the sets they had seen before.

When he joined up with Vic to ride back to the herd, he found out that Vic had also seen more tracks. They estimated that there were a minimum of ten men following them.

The valley was wide and gave them good visibility, but with the dips and ridges it was easy to keep out of sight. On occasion, they would see dust on the horizon. It was difficult to tell if it came from dust devils or riders.

Zac was at the end of the range, ahead of the herd, and was just about to turn back when he saw light reflect off something on the west ridge. He guided the piebald into a cut in the valley floor. He ground reined the horse and crawled up the side of the cut. At the upper edge he watched the west ridge.

The sun was hot and the air still as Zac watched. He saw the flash of light again. He guessed the source to be field glasses. Sweat trickled along his neck and down his back.

Finally, he saw what he was looking for. He could see movement and dust along the ridge. Someone was heading south and staying wide of the herd.

Zac slid back to the bottom of the cut and climbed into the saddle of the piebald. He headed across the valley toward the ridge. Zac had lined the flash with a jagged rock further up the ridge. He found the location of the man with the field glasses.

He scouted the area. Evidence showed

that the man had not been there long. He was probably riding when he'd noticed Zac. The trail went a little further into the hills. Zac followed, careful to keep his eyes open for any movement ahead.

Zac heard a whap and felt the shock of a bullet near his lower back, followed closely by the report of a rifle shot. The piebald leaped ahead, throwing him off its back. He landed face down on the ground as the horse galloped away.

He lay still, stunned from his head hitting the ground, struggling to breathe. The dust filled his nose and mouth. Zac forced himself to stay still. He lay in an open area and any movement could bring another shot.

As he lay there, he could feel something run down his lower side. He knew that he had been hit. If not by the bullet, then by fragments of it. The man he was tracking must have circled to check his back trail.

His lower back and side began to throb with pain. Zac was about to move when he heard gravel crunch under a boot. From the corner of his eye he could see a tooled leather boot with a large rowel spur.

The owner of the boot was about 20 feet away, and by its position he was crouching and leaning a bit forward. Zac guessed that he was wondering if he had hit his target well, or if he needed to shoot again. Zac sorely hoped that he thought the target was hit.

Zac heard a grunt, and the stalker straightened up and walked up to the front of him.

"You thought you could track me, Señor. Now, you are dead or dying."

The shooter shoved Zac onto his back with the toe of his boot. He barely saw the movement as the knife flashed, sinking to its hilt just above his belly button. Shocked, the man stumbled back into the sitting position.

Zac leaped up to tackle the man when his world spun, causing him to collapse short of his goal. Crying like a wounded animal, the man pulled the knife out and threw it to the side. Holding his stomach, with blood seeping out between his fingers, he stumbled away.

He lay on his back as he heard the sound of a departing horse. Zac could hear the eerie wail of the wounded man slowly fade as he rode away. The man had a stomach wound, and knew he would more than likely die.

Slowly, Zac got to his feet, steadying himself against a scrub pine. He had trouble focusing with both eyes. He felt his lower back. His shirt was covered with blood and dust. The wound did not feel too deep, but stung like crazy, throbbing with each beat of his heart.

He noticed the Good Knife lying in the dirt. He wiped its blade off in the sand and replaced it at the nape of his neck.

With one eye closed, he began to walk down the ridge, heading south to meet the herd. He had stumbled along about a half-hour before both eyes would focus.

His mouth was dry and his tongue felt thick. He selected a stone to suck on. It helped just a bit.

The sun was low in the sky, and he was still five miles away from the herd when he saw the black and white of his piebald. It stood head down, reins dragging. Zac had been riding the horse for several days now and had spent a lot of time gaining the horse's confidence. He spoke softly to the horse as he walked up.

Zac could see some blood on its rump. The piebald head came up and its nostril flared, snorting as it watched Zac come closer. It must have decided between wandering alone or being with the familiar man. The piebald whinnied and moved toward Zac.

It was well after dark when Zac rode up to the chuck wagon. He saw Dan and Vic talking with Rod. They had their horses saddled and were ready to come look for him.

"I'm alright," he called to them.

Dan and Vic came running to meet him. "Where have you been? We were about to give up on you coming back," Vic said.

"I ran into a little trouble with a dying Mexican," Zac replied. "His bullet glanced off the back of my saddle and fragments hit my back and my horse."

Zac had a fry pan and coffee pot tied to the back of his saddle. The fry pan now had a severely notched handle.

He walked to the fire and sat on a log next to it. Carla came from near the chuck wagon carrying a cloth and bandages. Dan had a pot of water heating next to the fire. He also had a hot cup of coffee for Zac.

Vic came back from treating the wound on the piebald's rump. He also gave the horse a quick rub down and some oats.

At the fire, he stopped to watch Carla clean and dress the gash on Zac's back. She was still wearing men's garb and had her hair tied back. He could have stood there for hours watching the smooth, gentle movements of her hands.

Zac sat with his shirt off and his lean muscles rippling with every move. Carla finished and headed back for the chuck wagon to put the extra bandages away. She hesitated briefly near Vic.

"Your cousin was lucky. If the Mexican had shot a couple of inches to the right, he would have taken one of Zac's kidneys out." Before leaving she added, "You be careful out there, Vic."

It was not the words that made him feel good, but the soft look on her face as she spoke. Again, he had hope that there could be more between them.

Rod, Eddie, Vic, and Dan sat around the fire, watching Zac finish up a plate of beans. He wiped the last of the juice with a piece of biscuit.

"I let the Mexican outthink me. I saw him on the ridge, and after he left I followed, hoping to find out where the rest were holding up. I should have known he would expect this."

"I managed to get my knife in him when he rolled me over. My aim was low and hit his stomach. It was only the fear that he was dying that made him run and not finish me off."

"They are getting bolder and getting ready to put a plan in operation. He would never have tried for me if the word was not out to start picking us off."

Rod turned to Eddie. "If they are planning to take action, where do you think it will happen?"

Eddie took the last drink of his coffee and shook out the cup. "The valley is wide here, and making a surprise attack will be difficult. Three to four days north of here we will be winding through some narrow passes. They will be able to pin us down and split the herd. I doubt they want to drive 4,000 head back south."

Eddie stood for a moment and looked toward the herd. "After killing those on the flanks, they will be able to drive the back half of the herd over those riding drag."

"The men in front will have 2,000 startled cattle in their way and that will prevent anyone from coming to support the back."

"Why do you think they will wait until the narrows?" Vic asked.

"Because that is the way I would have done it. And I know these men who follow us," Eddie replied bluntly.

The group broke up and headed for their bedrolls. No one asked Eddie how he knew these men. In the West, men had done many things. Sometimes, it was for the good of fellow man. Sometimes, fellow man was the victim. Men were judged by their actions. If they were honorable and trusting, their past was not questioned.

The plan was to slow the herd down until they could locate the camp of the men following them. The herd could not be stopped completely. There was not enough grazing in the valley.

Believing the attack would be in the direction of the narrows, according to Eddie, gave the cousins a much smaller area to search. There were a number of small canyons along the route that would make a good hideout. Once found, they would find a way to deal with the rustlers preemptively.

The narrows were now about three days ahead of the herd. That would be 40 miles, give or take. A man could ride the distance by horse in one day. But that would be riding without looking for anyone. Time was needed for searching. They took their blanket rolls and some food. The cousins would stay out until they found the hideout.

The eastern sky was just getting light when they rode out. Zac was on a dusty-colored black. His piebald needed a couple of days of rest.

The cousins now knew they were looking for men who would shoot on sight. Zac rode to the eastern ridge, while Dan and Vic rode to the west. They needed to get out of the valley before the sun came up.

The sun was just breaking the horizon when they entered the hills and blended into the terrain. Zac looked to the western ridge. He saw a slight movement just before his cousins disappeared behind a stand of pine.

He played yesterday's events over in his mind. He realized how close he'd came to being killed. He also had the cold understanding that his actions had probably killed a man. He could still remember the wailing of the man as he'd ridden away.

Dan and Vic stopped in the stand of pines. "We need to split up to cover more area," Dan suggested.

"I want to ride a bit south and then work my way north, Dan. You go north and we can meet up around midday."

Dan glanced at the eastern ridge. The sun was large and bright, just above the horizon. He said a brief prayer for his cousin's safety. Moving north, he rode out of the pines on his chestnut. He looked back and saw that Vic was already gone.

It did not take long for Vic to pick up tracks. Those watching must be quite confident in their venture. They knew that their presence was known to the herd crew.

Vic worried that the group might not have a central camp, but planned to come together when the herd entered the narrow pass area. The rustlers shooting at them would indicate their plan was in the final stages. They were confident that they had the upper hand.

Vic stopped his bay next to a small pool of water and let it drink while he chewed some beef jerky. He took a drink from his canteen and hung it back onto his saddle. It was time to work his way back to Dan.

Dan was following two sets of tracks. He recognized them as the horses ridden by Juan and Filipe. Rather than follow the tracks and give them a chance to spring a trap, Dan rode up to a high point on the ridge and kept himself and his horse just below the skyline.

Wrapping the chestnut's reins around a stunted evergreen, he settled down to watch the valley. Dust was rising in the south. He knew that would be the herd. His view from the ridge was easily a day's drive for the herd.

Dan was holding a small cylindrical tube in his right hand. He extended it with his left. Before they'd left the herd, Rod had given him the brass spyglass. The patina on the spyglass would prevent reflection.

Dan hooded the lens with his hand as he slowly scanned the valley. He spent most of an hour looking for any sign of riders or smoke from a campfire. He was just about to move to another spot when his search was rewarded. North, along the same ridge as he was on, he caught sight of a wisp of smoke.

It disappeared before he could pick out some landmarks. After another 10 minutes he saw it again. This time he lined it up with a jagged, forked peak just beyond the smoke and a lightning-struck pine stump before. He estimated that the smoke was just less than two miles away.

Dan picked out a narrow ledge below him that would allow him to travel faster and block out any view of him from the camp. He would come out just short of the stump.

The chestnut proved to be a good mountain horse. It walked confidently along the ledge. In some cases, Dan's left stirrup would scrape against the rock wall while he looked down a steep cliff on the right.

Shortly, the pine stump was in sight. Dan swung down from his horse and led it toward the landmark. Once there, he aligned himself with the jagged, forked peak. Between the two, he could see a leaning boulder. He was now less than a mile from the smoke. While he could not see it anymore, he knew the trail would be fresh.

He led his horse to the leaning boulder. The sun was high, making the heat on the ridge stifling. Dan could feel the tension in his stomach. He wished that he had Zac's stealth. Yet even Zac had been tricked following these men.

Dan swung back into the saddle. The hot leather burnt the insides of his thighs. The reward for walking his horse, Dan thought. He could see a point of rock jutting out between him and the jagged peak. The source of the smoke would have come from just beyond that area.

Dan planned his moves carefully. He removed the loop from his Colt. He decided to leave the rifle in its scabbard for the time being. At close quarters his Colt would be a better weapon. If he fought from a distance he would have adequate time to reach the Winchester.

He knew that he would be safe riding on this side of the point of rock. He would then have to decide the best route after rounding the point. He urged the horse forward.

A hawk shrieked above him as it rode

the rising heat waves and searched for a meal. Dan could see antelope in the valley floor, grazing and playing in the heat.

Dan continued on around the rock. His chestnut stepped off a shelf and the loose rock slid from under its back hoof. It jumped ahead and scrambled onto solid ground. Dan had to struggle to keep his seat. He looked ahead and went cold inside. He was facing six Mexican riders who were 30 feet from him.

Dan let the chestnut keep walking as he stared at the riders. A quick survey told him that Juan or Filipe were not among them. He closed the distance to just under ten feet.

"Look, boys," the overweight man in the middle scoffed. "We have ourselves a pigeon here."

Dan had often listened to the stories from his Uncle Karl about his time in the War Between the States. He said that during an unexpected confrontation against superior numbers, the first few seconds are the key to escape. It is the time that your enemy has the least control of the situation. They expect you to freeze due to their numbers. And most important of all, they are as surprised as you.

The fat man started to speak again as he reached for his pistol. Dan drew the Colt and fired in one motion. It is said that you hit what you are looking at. His bullet entered the fat man's mouth and exited out the back of his head, spraying brains and blood over the rump of his horse.

Dan spurred the chestnut forward at one of the riders on the left while he fired into the body of a man on the right. The Mexican riders were in confusion. Dan was in the middle of the group and if they shot and missed the bullet would hit one of their own.

Their leader fell back off his horse, dead before he hit the ground. The man on the right was hit by Dans' bullet just above the left hip. The man and horse on the left rolled into the dirt from the chestnut's charge.

Instinct made the two remaining men duck for cover, expecting bullets to be coming their way. Dan rode hard and low, putting distance between the riders and himself. He saw a pine-covered hillside just below and put the chestnut off the side of the ledge. Sliding on its haunches, it scrambled down the steep hill.

Dan heard gunshots behind him. He was now well below them and they were shooting high. He had slipped his Colt back in his holster and was doing everything he could to stay on the chestnut and control its descent.

Reaching the trees, he turned the chestnut parallel to the hill and entered the pines. Dan leaped from the horse, grabbing his Winchester.

He moved back to get a view of the ledge above him. He saw the two men holding rifles looking for a glimpse of him to shoot at. Dan sighted on the man on the left. Adjusting for the uphill shot, he squeezed off the shot.

The bullet ricocheted off the ledge next to the man's boot. Rock sprayed his leg and he yelped and jumped back. The two men ran for their mounts and leaped into the saddles. It went against Dan's grain to punish an animal for the wrong doings of its master, but he felt he had no choice. As the two men spurred their horses heading south, Dan took sight on the lead horse. He squeezed off his second shot. The horse faltered briefly and then began to run. It quickly lagged the second horse. Dan knew that the man would soon be afoot.

Dan could see the horse knocked down by the chestnut standing a bit to the north. He could not see the man he had knocked down, or the second man he'd shot at. It would be foolish to try and climb back up the slope to see what had happened to them. A wounded man with a rifle is still dangerous.

He caught movement out of the corner of his eye. Someone was sneaking along the ledge in front of the point of rock. The man was not moving away from the confrontation, but rather toward it.

Dan retrieved the spyglass from his horse and trained it on the area. He finally picked out the moving form of a man. It was Vic!

Dan raised his Colt and fired two quick warning shots. He saw Vic stop and look in his direction. Dan motioned in front of Vic, not daring to expose himself too much. In turn, Vic waved and moved slowly. Vic disappeared as he entered the area where the men would have been. For a long moment Dan waited, and then Vic appeared at the ledge and waved for him to join him.

Taking the reins of the chestnut, Dan worked his way back up to the ledge. He gained the ledge near the standing horse. Dan caught up the loose horse's reins and led the two horses back toward Vic.

Dan found Vic leaning over the wounded man, applying a bandage to stop the bleeding. Dan could see the other man who'd fallen with the charged horse. He lay dead in a heap with his neck twisted, almost looking behind him. No doubt when the horse had rolled on him, he'd broken his neck.

The fat man Dan shot first lay face down with the back of his head a bloody mass. Dan felt his stomach turn a bit when he looked at the man. He was glad that he could not see the face. The wounded man was of a smaller stature. He had a thin moustache and his face was twisted in pain.

"He confirmed my suspicions," Vic said as he worked on the Mexican. "This man's name is Pablo. I told him if he answered my questions correctly we would help him. If I thought he was not telling the truth, I would leave him for the coyotes tonight."

"What were your suspicions?" Dan asked.

"He confirmed that there is not a central camp. That is why we were finding lots of tracks and no meeting of them in one direction. They were told to travel in small groups until we got into the narrow passes. Eddie was right. They are supposed to come together on the east and west sides above the pass and kill as many men as possible while splitting the herd in half."

"They only wanted part of the herd. It would be difficult to drive the whole herd back south and there would not be enough food left for all the cattle."

Pablo spoke in broken English, "Señor, I no lie to you. You not leave me?"

Vic assured him, "You kept your part of our bargain. We will take you with us. We have a man named Eduardo Garcia that will want to talk to you."

Dan saw the man's face pale, and his eyes showed pure terror.

"You have met Eduardo before?" Dan asked Pablo.

"Don't worry Pablo, we won't let Eddie hurt you too much. You just tell him and Mr. Tilison what you told me and you will be okay," Vic assured the frightened man.

Vic dragged the two dead men to a

depression near a rock ledge. He and Dan piled rocks on the bodies. Vic then took the horse Dan had gotten and rode to get his horse.

He had been only half a mile away when the shooting started. He'd ridden hard toward the gunfire. He had just hidden his horse and started on foot when he'd heard Dan's rifle shots.

The two men had come spurring their horses past Vic, who had ducked behind some boulders. The lagging rider had yelled for the other man to wait for him. Vic had seen the blood spraying out of the side of the man's horse.

When he'd gotten to the scene of the fight, he'd found Pablo dragging himself away, looking for a place to hide.

Dan and Vic rode their horses to the middle of the valley, leading Pablo's horse. Their hope was that Zac would catch sight of them and realize they were heading back to the herd.

Pablo groaned with every step of his horse. His hip might have been broken by Dan's bullet. Vic had tied his hands to the front of his saddle. It was as much to keep him from falling off his horse as to stop him from fleeing.

Dan sat quietly, staring at the horizon.

"You want to talk, Dan?" Vic asked.

"I never killed a man before. Now I

have the credit for two men dead."

"They gave you no choice," Vic argued.

"Killing came too easy, Vic. I hardly remember drawing my gun. There wasn't even fear. I remember feeling excitement."

"You remember my father talking about the war. You were prepared. You knew what had to be done. He had been in the same type of situation. The exhilaration you felt was knowing how to survive," Vic said, trying to give Dan another explanation.

Dan looked at Vic and smiled. "Maybe."

Pablo was slumped in the saddle, and had passed out from the pain by the time they reached the herd. The chuck wagon was already setting up for supper. Vic and Dan carried Pablo from the horse and laid him onto some blankets.

Rod and Eddie rode up. "We noticed you come in. What do you have there?" Rod asked.

Vic explained what he had confirmed from Pablo, that the men after the herd wouldn't come together until they reached the narrows. He then told them about Dan's confrontation with the six riders. As he spoke, Rod looked over at Dan with admiration. Carla was standing beside the chuck wagon, listening and staring wide-eyed.

Eddie slapped Dan on the back. "You did a fine job, my friend. This Pablo looks familiar."

Dan agreed. "He should. Just the mention of your name scared him half to death."

"There are many such men who live with the same fear, amigo," Eddie said, with a prideful smile.

Vic and Dan sat eating a late supper. Ling had kept the pot of beans hot next to the fire. Vic glanced over at Eddie talking with Pablo. As they spoke, Eddie carried his whip and slowly slid it through his hand. Pablo was physically shaking and nodding in agreement to the questions Eddie asked.

"I am sure glad Eddie Garcia is on our side," Vic said.

CHAPTER NINE

The next morning Carla Tilison came around the chuck wagon, chewing on a biscuit with honey. She was wearing her hair up under her flat-brimmed hat. She had straight-legged men's trousers worn over snakeskin boots, and a plaid wool shirt. A tan deerskin vest was worn open over the wool shirt.

Vic was rolling up his blankets. He watched Carla as she walked toward him. He knew the goal was to make her look like one of the men, but she was far too much of a woman to convince anyone otherwise.

Carla stopped in front of Vic and stood with her hands on her hips. "Nice job on the bedroll, cowboy," she teased.

Vic felt his face growing red. He was frustrated. Usually, he had no problem talking and joking with the opposite sex. For some reason Carla left him tongue-tied.

"I, uh . . . thanks," he mumbled.

"Rod sent me to find you. He wants you and your cousins to meet with him right after breakfast." Turning on her heel, Carla walked back toward the chuck wagon.

Just before rounding the corner of the wagon, she glanced back and caught Vic watching her. Vic angrily finished tying the bedroll, hearing her giggle as she disappeared. He slammed his bed roll into the hoodlum wagon with such force it made Pep jump.

It was just full morning light when the three looked for Rod. Ling had porridge with maple syrup for the morning meal. The coffee was strong, and they each took an extra cup with them.

"She just makes me so damn. . . I can't explain it," Vic muttered.

"I think our cousin is in love, Dan," Zac laughed.

"Damn it, Zac," Vic bristled, "I have never been in love, and if this is it I am not liking the feeling."

The cousins were surprised to find the two Texans and Kelly Walsh at the meeting. Eddie was seated next to Rod. Abe stood rolling a smoke with one hand. Jack was squatting down, poking at the ground with a stick. Abe handed the makings over to Dan as they walked up.

"Thanks, Abe, don't mind if I do," Dan said as he accepted the bag of tobacco.

Rod stood up and looked over the men. "The five of you were chosen for what we will be facing the next couple of days. As you know, there are those who would like to take part of the herd away from us. We will be entering the narrow part of the valley tomorrow morning."

"It's believed that it's the area they will strike. Eddie knows the narrows and has a plan to stop an attack on the herd."

Eddie stood confidently, his shirt open, exposing his hair-covered chest. He held his ever-present bullwhip in one hand and his other hand rested on his gun butt. He cleared his throat and picked up the stick Jack had dropped. He quickly drew the layout of the narrow valley in the dirt for the men to look at.

Pointing to the west side of the valley he began. "We need to set up a defense in the narrows before the Comancheros move in. I will be covering the west bank with Vic and Dan. Rod will be on the east side with Abe and Jack. We need to be in place by midday today.

"Zac and Kelly, you will be riding the area southwest of the herd. Your job will be to harass and delay those coming to take over the herd after the attack."

"Once the herd is through the narrows, we will join forces and stop anyone from following the herd."

"The men after the cattle will not hesitate to kill anyone. We are not many, and do not have the manpower to take prisoners. Stay sharp, amigos."

The meeting broke up, with everyone understanding that the instructions were shoot-to-kill. Those coming had already shown that they were ruthless.

Dan and Vic got their horses and joined Eddie. The Texans rode away with Rod.

Zac was happy to see the piebald was fit to ride. The rump had a gash that had been treated with axle grease to keep the flies off.

Kelly Walsh was an easygoing Irishman with a quick smile. His demeanor could make others underestimate his abilities. Zac had watched Kelly work around the cattle, or stalk wild game. Zac was pleased to have him as a partner.

Dan rode on the left side of Eddie Garcia. He was smoking a cigarette and watching the horizon.

"I didn't see Pablo anywhere this morning, Eddie," he said indifferently.

"He is no doubt with his people," Eddie responded. "The wound was bad and his days left short."

Vic looked at Eddie riding easily in the saddle. He wondered if Eddie meant with

Pablo's ancestors or his friends. The words "we do not have the manpower to take prisoners" echoed in his ears.

Zac and Kelly knew that most of the tracks seen had come from the southwest. They cut a route that would put them about a mile behind the herd as it reached the narrows. They noticed a ridge that would give them a good field of vision to the herd and well behind the point they were at. Without a spoken word, the two men split up to cover a wider area and disappeared into the hills.

Rod and the Texans arrived at the east side of the narrows and looked over the best locations to attack the right flank of the herd. Rod motioned them to spread out and take cover on nearby high ground.

The sun was high and the day was hot. Abe and Jack took advantage of any available shade. They knew that these same spots would be sought by those planning to attack.

Eddie pulled up his horse. He took a drink from his canteen and then wiped his mouth with the back of his hand.

"You men should know that we will be coming on to Juan and Filipe near the ledge you see in the distance. They have been watching our progress along the valley."

Dan and Vic looked at each other with concern. How would Eddie know this? Was this some type of trap? If a trap, why would he tip them off?

Eddie continued. "We have the upper hand when we meet them. They think I am bringing the two of you to them for slaughter. Juan and Filipe will have four to six others with them. I will need you to ride just ahead of me as we come up to them. They will be relaxed, waiting for me to kill you both."

Vic felt the hair stand up on the back of his neck. His stomach was queasy. He looked at Dan for some kind of lead.

"How can we be sure you're not planning to follow through with killing us? Why do you know so much about their plan?" Dan asked.

"Both good questions," Eddie answered. "You won't know for sure until I make my move. Once I fire, you both draw and shoot anyone on the side you are on. You should know I was offered good money by those wanting to steal the herd."

"Did you take the money?" Vic quipped.

"I took money," Eddie confirmed, "but not from them. Mr. Tilison offered me more. That I took."

The three approached the ledge. Vic and Dan could see horsemen waiting in a grove of aspen. Eddie began to slow just a bit, allowing Vic and Dan to move ahead a half a horse length. As they closed, the cousins moved out, giving them a broader front.

Eddie stopped short of the horsemen. Dan and Vic could not see him behind them.

Vic had never felt so exposed to danger before in his life. He felt sweat run down the side of his face and the back of his neck. He desperately wanted to wipe it, but any move on their part could start the gunplay.

Vic could see Dan out of the corner of his eye. He was showing no emotion. It appeared that he was sitting loose in the saddle.

"Señor, buen dia," Eddie welcomed Juan and Filipe.

Juan smiled broadly, clenching a cheroot in his gold-capped teeth. "Filipe did not think you would come, jefe."

"That is because Filipe does not know me. When I say I will come, I come," Eddie assured them.

Listening to them, Vic's life passed before his eyes. He could not believe they had walked into this like lambs to the slaughter. His muscles tightened as he prepared to react in some way.

A whip shot out on his left side, wrapping around Filipe's neck. A quick jerk broke the man's neck. There was a gunshot, and Juan fell from his saddle. Vic could see Dan's Colt in his hand, bucking as he fired. Vic drew his gun and swung the barrel at the man furthest to the right and squeezed off a shot.

The air erupted with the roar of gunfire. As quickly as it started, it was over and the gun smoke hung heavily in the air. In front of the three men lay eight dead or dying Comancheros.

One of the men Vic had shot was crawling toward some cover. Eddie urged his horse forward and stopped above the man. He put another bullet into the wounded man, finishing what Vic had started.

Vic sat on the bay, fighting back the feeling of nausea. Just moments before, he had killed and wounded two men. He had then watched the wounded man executed. He looked at Dan. He was ejecting the empty shells from his gun and reloading. Dan's face had no expression.

Vic turned the bay away from the mayhem and gave the appearance that he was looking for any men who might be coming from another direction. He heard a horse coming toward him. He looked up at Dan.

"Vic, it is important to remember that these men came here to kill us. We are in a war with them. What we just did was done in fair play. They had every intention of killing us," Dan pointed out.

Concern suddenly showed in Dan's eyes. "You were hit, Vic." Dan was pointing at Vic's side.

Vic felt his side and his hand came away wet with blood. He could now feel the burning where the bullet had grazed him. "It's nothing, Dan, just a scratch."

Vic couldn't believe he had been hit and hadn't felt it before Dan pointed it out. He heard Eddie riding up.

"I see they got some lead into you, amigo. Best get a bandage on it before it draws flies. We have much to do yet before the sun goes down."

* * *

Rod heard the gunfire from across the valley. He sincerely hoped Vic and Dan were okay. He heard horses coming from the south. The riders were hurrying. No doubt they were late getting into position. The sounds of their horses would have prevented them from hearing the shooting across the valley. As the men rounded the hillside, the Texans opened fire on them.

The riders' horses began to buck and snort. The men fighting to stay in the saddles were shouting and grabbing for their guns. A horse plunged forward and fell mortally wounded, throwing the rider over its head. There were ten riders in the group.

Rod raised his rifle and joined the Texans, picking out targets and squeezing off shots. He could see men falling, their horses stomping on them. There were the shrill cries of the horses and men. As quickly as they had appeared, the riders who were able to, rode back out of sight. Two of the men without horses, and sporting wounds, ducked behind available cover and started returning fire in the direction of the Texans.

Rod could see one of the men's legs sticking out from behind the rocks. Taking careful aim, he put a bullet through the man's calf. The leg was jerked back accompanied by a yell of pain. The other man ducked and ran for better cover. A shot from Abe cut the man down in mid-stride.

The wounded man began to shout that he was giving up. Rod remembered what Eddie had said. He knew that he could not stand by and watch a wounded man be shot while giving up.

"Abe, Jack, don't shoot him!" Rod shouted. "You below, toss out your gun and crawl out with your hands showing!"

The man tossed out his gun and dragged himself from behind the rocks. Looking around for any of the other men, Rod worked his way down to the man. He heard one of the Texans coming down.

"Jack is covering us in case any of the others come back. You done right, boss, not killing him," Abe said.

The man had two additional wounds along with the leg wound. One on his hip was slight. One in his shoulder was more serious. Rod wrapped the shoulder and calf to slow the bleeding. Abe went to get one of the horses that wasn't injured.

"Do you have anyone in the area that can help you?" Rod asked.

Breathing heavily and wincing with pain, the man nodded. "I have an uncle east of here. He begged me not to join these men. I wanted to get money for him."

"If we let you go, can you make it to him?" Rod asked.

"I think so, señor."

"I do not want to see you again. If you know any more that might be coming, tell them to go back. The herd will not be given up," Rod warned.

Abe and Rod helped the man into the saddle and watched him ride east, slouching over the saddle horn. They then moved back into the rocks, watching for any more riders.

* * *

Zac sat watching, taking advantage of the shade of a gnarled pine. His horse was hidden deeper in the rocks on a patch of grass. He looked to his left. Kelly had disappeared into some brush.

He could see dust rising south of them. The herd entered the narrows north of them. Zac's eyes strained to get a glimpse of the riders from the south. He thought he heard some gunfire a half hour earlier. He wasn't able to determine the exact direction it had come from.

He suddenly caught movement to his left. Kelly was repositioning to intercept the riders. Zac moved down the slope to make sure that he was in range as the riders passed. He was just able to make out the shapes of the riders rounding the hill.

There were about twenty of them. Zac knew that they could not kill or wound twenty men on horseback. The hope was to scatter and slow them, allowing the herd to move through the narrows.

He had moved below Kelly and to his left. He noticed Kelly signal him. Kelly would be in range first, so he was letting Zac know that he would hold his fire until Zac fired.

From below, Zac was getting a better look at the riders. They looked more like drovers than gunmen. They wore chaps and had riatas on their saddles. It did not appear that any had rifles. Most wore handguns.

Zac made a quick decision. He aimed at the lead horse and squeezed off a shot. The bullet burned the horse, causing it to leap, twist and stumble. He continued to shoot near the riders, trying his best not to take any center body shots at anyone. He could hear Kelly shooting. He saw one of the riders fall from his horse, bounce on the ground and leap up running to climb up behind a fellow rider.

His assessment was correct. These men were not gunmen, and once fired at they turned and put distance between them and the unseen rifles. They would not be coming back to drive the herd.

Zac and Kelly collected their horses and rode hard to catch up to the herd. There were three men from the herd to their left. They were looking for something on the ground. Kelly and Zac pulled up next to them. The looks on their faces were frantic.

"They got Carla! The sons-o-bitches got her!" a dust-covered cowboy shouted.

Quickly, Zac and Kelly were brought up to date. Carla had been helping drive the cattle and riding left flank. Some riders came out of a ravine and grabbed her. The kidnappers rode west and the men were looking for their tracks.

A short, stocky cowboy swore, "That damn Cal and Wally were riding drag and didn't lift a finger to help her. They claimed they couldn't see through the dust. We were about a half mile up and we saw it. We couldn't get here before they disappeared into the hills."

"You guys go back and keep the herd going through the narrows," Zac instructed. "Kelly, you cover their back trail. I'll go and get Carla back."

Without further word, Zac whirled the piebald and headed for the hills, scanning the ground for tracks. His face was hard as stone, his stomach tight with concern. What kind of men would grab the girl? It was a question he did not want answered.

He picked up the tracks of her buckskin being crowded by two other horses. He let the piebald run. As though it understood the urgency, it went at a mile-eating gallop.

Once in the hills Zac found an area where Carla had tried to make a break. It was evident that her buckskin was worn down from driving the cattle and was being corralled by two fresher horses. A third rider had joined the others. He had been waiting for them.

Zac had been tracking them at a reckless speed when he noticed a change in the way they were moving. He slowed the piebald. He noticed that the buckskin was now being led. Carla's hands must be tied.

He saw that one of the horsemen had moved away, heading for rocks on higher ground. Zac was crossing an open area when he saw a flash of light and threw himself from the piebald. He felt the bullet tug at his shirt as he went over, followed by the report of a rifle. As he went over, he grabbed the stirrup of his horse.

Startled, the piebald ran forward, dragging Zac. The rifleman had made the mistake of believing he had hit Zac and that his target was now being pulled by the horse with a foot in the stirrup. As the horse passed behind some low brush, Zac released the stirrup and rolled clear of the running horse.

He lay watching for the shooter. He heard him move before he could see him. The man was cautiously climbing down to make sure Zac was dead. He lay flat, looking through the scrub brush. He fought back the urge to sneeze from the dust in his nose. The heel of his hand was scraped and stinging.

He had not removed the loop from his gun and found it still in his holster. He drew the gun and watched for the shooter to appear. The man suddenly emerged. He had his eye on the piebald and was slowly moving in that direction.

Zac put his Colt back in its holster and began to move around the back of the shooter. He closed the distance quickly, moving on silent feet. He grabbed the man from the back and sunk the Good Knife into him under his ribcage, thrusting up.

The man grunted and struggled briefly. His legs suddenly collapsed and Zac let him fall face down in the sandy soil. Zac wiped the blade in the dirt. Tossing the man's gun away from the body, Zac did not stop to confirm a kill. He caught the piebald and continued to track the remaining men who had Carla.

It was dark when Zac reached them. It appeared that they were not worried about being followed. The two were cooking supper. Zac ground reined the piebald and moved toward the camp.

He could see Carla sitting on the

ground, tied hand and foot. The two men were laughing and talking as they pointed at the girl. Their language was Spanish, which Zac understood.

The third man was expected to come in any time. There was a single shot and that meant their friend had scored with the first shot. The two figured he was still watching to make sure no one else followed.

They joked about the money they would get selling the blond girl. There were people who would pay well for the prize. It was more than they would have gotten from grabbing the herd.

Zac went back to the piebald and swung into the saddle. The men were expecting their friend. Riding into the camp without hesitation would make them believe the friend was joining them.

"Poco, you sure took your time," a short fat man called out.

He grunted a reply and guided the horse with his knees. When the firelight exposed the black and white piebald the two men cried out and grabbed for their guns. Zac had his Winchester Model 1873 out and ready.

He fired at the closer man, shooting the rifle one-handed. Swinging the piebald with his knees, he lined up and shot the fat man in the center of his dirty shirt.

The shots were still echoing in the hills

when the two men hit the ground, never to rise again. Zac leaped from the piebald and knelt beside Carla, cutting her loose. Her hair was disheveled and her face covered with dust. She had a bruise on the right cheek. No doubt a well-placed punch when she was trying to escape.

The defiance in her eyes disappeared and they filled with tears. She fought them back, but finally gave up and hung her head and cried.

"You're safe now, Carla," Zac assured her. "These men have grabbed their last woman."

Zac saddled her buckskin and rode away from the camp with her after pushing sand over the fire.

The moon was bright over the valley as they rode after the herd. There was a group of riders coming toward them. Zac could make out Rod and Vic in the lead. Zac called out to them.

In a cloud of dust, the riders surrounded the two. Rod hugged Carla, almost pulling her from her saddle. He kept saying how scared he was that she couldn't be found. Vic sat looking at Carla.

As the group rode back toward the herd, Vic pulled up alongside Carla. He had thought killing a man was the worst that could happen until he found out Carla had been grabbed. He wasn't sure life was worth living without seeing her smile.

He rode, trying to think of something to say to Carla. She looked at him and smiled. He saw the bruise on her cheek.

"I'm sorry I wasn't there to stop the men from hurting you," he said lamely.

"I knew you or your cousins would come and get me," she replied.

They rode through the narrows until they caught up with the herd. Carla and Vic rode side-by-side the entire way.

CHAPTER TEN

Eddie assigned extra guards that night, but was confident that the danger was over. The herd was in Colorado. Their next destination was Pueblo. They would be restocking the chuck wagon. The herd was in fair condition. Grazing for the cattle had been marginal. Water had been good.

Two nights after the attack on the herd, Rod Tilison met with Dan, Vic, and Zac. He had asked them to tell him what they had seen during the attack. He patiently listened as each told him in detail their experiences. When they concluded, he filled their cups with coffee and thought for a moment.

"I hope you men don't judge me too severely for hiring a man like Eddie Garcia to ramrod this drive," he began. "I do not agree with his methods, and in hindsight I should have probably looked elsewhere. I can tell you this: If he was not working for us, we would have been fighting Eddie for the herd. I can also let you know that Eddie will be leaving us in Denver. He wants to be south for the winter."

"We understand why you hired Eddie," Dan said. "No doubt, your hiring Eddie saved many of the lives of those driving the herd."

"You and your father have been more than fair with us," Vic added.

Rod looked over at Cal and Wally lounging next to the fire. "I will also be cutting some of the men in Denver. At that point, I shouldn't need you guarding the herd. I will need you to help with the drive. You will be working for Kelly. He will be taking Eddie's place."

Zac looked at Vic and Dan. "I don't think we have a problem with that. Kelly is a top hand and someone you can trust to cover your back."

Vic and Dan nodded in agreement.

"One other thing," Rod said. "I would like you to consider helping with the cattle this winter. Your pay will stay at $40 a month and in the spring there will be a bonus based on how the cattle winter."

The cousins had thought about the search for the gold this time of year. It would be late fall when they got to Wyoming. Passes in the mountains would be snowed in, so any travel would be limited. Working for the Tilison's would solve finding a place to winter.

Dan was the first to answer Rod. "If the others would let me speak for them, I think we would like that fine."

Rod smiled. "You know, it wasn't by accident that I was on the train with you. My father read about your capture of the Alan gang. He asked me to find out if the story writer was embellishing the event or accurate."

"I found out that your actions had exceeded the writer's account. I learned about your fathers saving your grandmother's home. I found out about your father, Vic, during the War Between the States. I even learned a thing or two about your grandfather, Oli August."

"Your families' willingness to help others, and bravery when facing danger told me you were men we wanted on the drive. One old man I spoke with was Jacob Wolfe. He had nothing good to say about you or your family, except . . . that if I wanted three of the best fighting men in Iowa, you men were it."

The mention of Jacob Wolfe's name brought back memories of the constant conflict that the Wolfe brothers had had with their grandfather. Jacob's brother Tate had sent his sons with their fathers on a cattle drive with instructions to make sure it was not successful. Both had died, one by the

Comanches, and the other by the hand of Karl when he'd tried to rob gold from them.

Tate Wolfe had been a broken man after the loss of his sons. He had known that he was responsible. He had let his businesses go. Just under a year later, downstream from the August home, on the banks of Turkey River, he had ended his life with a single-shot dueling pistol.

Jacob Wolfe had then sold off the brothers' assets and lived quietly on the edge of town. He was often seen sitting on his porch, half-passed out after he had too much to drink. His recommendations to Rod were the last thing Dan, Vic, or Zac had expected.

Pueblo was situated on the banks of the Arkansas River. It had first been settled in 1842 and called El Pueblo. It was now a mixture of brick and wood structures, as well as adobe buildings.

The herd was kept well outside of the town. Ling and Kelly went into town to purchase goods. Dan and Vic began to take their turns in rotation driving the cattle. Zac helped with the horse remuda, taking the kinks out of the wilder stock. Each day, they would scout around the herd before bedding them down, to make sure there were not any outsiders watching them.

Dan had sent a letter to Mary before leaving Santa Fe. He asked Kelly to check if any mail had come to Pueblo. Vic and Zac had also sent letters to their families from Santa Fe, but they were not expecting any replies.

Ling returned with the chuck wagon. Kelly had purchased some replacement horses, which remained in Pueblo. He needed men to ride into town and drive them back. Rod sent Zac and Dan. Nudging Zac, Dan pointed to Vic helping Carla, Ling, and Pep sort the supplies and repair items between the chuck wagon and hoodlum wagon.

Dan was glad to see Vic laughing and being more relaxed. He had worried about Vic after the confrontation in the narrows. To know that he had killed his first man, and then watch Eddie kill the one he'd wounded, in cold blood, had left him sleeping restlessly. Vic did not want to talk about it, and he made sure he stayed clear of Eddie Garcia as much as he could.

It was mid-September when they left Pueblo. There had been no mail. It would be a 10-day drive to Denver. The plan was to spend a week letting the herd rest before pushing on to Cheyenne. The final destination was a week's drive north of Cheyenne. They should arrive at the ranch by the end of October.

Cal and Wally were more difficult to be around than ever. It was obvious that they were not looked at in the same way as the August cousins. They did their job with very little enthusiasm. Cal was quick to pick an argument with other drovers. Both were still making $30 a month.

Vic kept his distance from Cal. Not that he feared him, but there was nothing to be proven by fighting Cal. Vic had one confrontation with him two days out of Pueblo. He went to get a horse from the remuda. There were several horses tied and ready for the day's work. Vic saw a roan he liked to ride. He walked toward it and Cal brushed by, bumping him and grabbing the roan's halter rope.

"I believe you saw me heading for that horse, Cal," Vic said in a cold and even voice.

The two men stood glaring at each other. Vic was sure that things were about to get bloody. Incredibly, Cal threw the rope down and stomped off to get another horse. He watched what he had always thought of as a big man back down. Cal was only big in size. The drive had taken much of the aggressiveness and self-assurance out of him.

Vic was enjoying Carla's company and was finding it easier to talk with her. She was back to wearing ladies' clothes and rode in the chuck wagon with Ling most of the time. He knew he was in love, but had little to offer Carla. Vic decided to enjoy her company during the drive and when it was over, she would go one way, he another. This realization made him moody and wishing that Cal would start something.

RETURN TO OLI'S GOLD

The grazing was a bit better between Pueblo and Denver. The 4,000 cattle, plus riding stock, created a wide scar on the high desert landscape. The grass was mostly dry and brown. It still made acceptable grazing. The first frost of the season had not hit yet, so other succulent plants were still available.

Ling had picked up chickens in Pueblo and treated the crew to chicken and biscuits for supper. It was a welcome change from the routine of steak and beans. Zac had brought down a large female elk some days before. While the elk tasted very good, it did not compare to the evening of chicken and biscuits.

There was one morning when Vic came in exhausted from riding watch on the herd. They had some wolves that were determined to make some of the weaker ones their meal. After four hours of keeping the wolves at bay, he was ready to settle down to a hot bowl of porridge.

As he rode in he could smell bacon. He knew this meant that breakfast would be leftover beans and bacon. Carla was standing next to the chuck wagon as he walked up from dropping off his horse. He tossed down his saddle, with the intention of grabbing a few minutes sleep after breakfast before going back to the drive.

"You do look a sight, Mr. August," she taunted.

"If that is how I look, Miss Tilison, I want you to know I feel twice as bad."

"Well," she said, "maybe this will perk you up, cowboy."

Carla had set up a table on a round flat rock. She had bacon, biscuits with jam, and . . Vic couldn't believe it, eggs!

Smiling from ear to ear, she watched Vic dig into his breakfast. Carla knew that the others would kid him later on, but it was a pure pleasure watching him enjoy his meal.

Carla had a secret that she had not shared with Vic. Her father would be waiting for them in Denver. He would be meeting the drive and sending her east to attend school. Carla doubted that she would ever see Vic again after leaving. She felt very close to Vic, but did not dare let him know. To admit how she felt to Vic would hurt too much when she had to leave. It would hurt them both, she was sure.

* * *

Vic, Dan, and Zac sat on a rise, watching the cattle strung out over a mile as they slowly wormed their way east of Denver. The South Platte River ran below Denver. Their horses stomped and snorted with impatience as the men stared. The sun had been up for three hours, but the air was still cool.

RETURN TO OLI'S GOLD

Each knew that they were only a few miles from the point where their grandfather had left the wagon train. Vic carried the ledger and had been studying it for the past couple of weeks. It read like a diary, calling out landmarks and events of each day. The men's plan was to keep track of the landmarks as they went.

The cousins spent time away from the rest, looking at their copies of the map. Vic had made a rough estimate of some of the landmarks on his map. Without any scale on the map locations, he added marks and numbered them with days' travel. This was similar to the original map maker's notes of days walking.

Information was gotten about the Stinking Water River and determined that it flowed into the Big Horn River, which meant that their grandfather had gone up into Wyoming. The task of finding the location of the gold was becoming overwhelming.

There was a wide expanse of grass east of Denver. The cattle would have to be moved each day, or the area would be over-grazed.

When the wind blew, which was almost every day, the tumble weeds would roll across the landscape, dropping seeds for next season. The first time Dan's chestnut saw one, it almost unseated him when it jumped.

Eddie was paid for his services, and he left with three of the Mexican drovers. The

Texans planned to stay with the drive until Cheyenne. Surprisingly, Cal and Wally let Rod know that they were leaving the drive in Denver. Both drew their pay and kept their horses.

Rod had planned to let them go regardless. He also asked the two men who had challenged Zac early in the drive to leave. It was not for their confrontation with Zac, but rather that they tended to be disagreeable and dodged work whenever possible.

Bill Tilison met the herd in Denver. He wanted to look them over and then had business in Kansas City. He was a tall man, with a barrel chest and a booming voice. His clothes were tailored and he had a head of bushy gray hair. His square chin was punctuated by a dimple.

The cattle were a bit thin. Around five percent of them were lost during the drive. Some were lost due to injury, some to wolves, and others hadn't had the stamina to make the trip.

Denver was located in the high desert, over 5000 feet elevation. The cattle were just east of town and were busy grazing on grasses consisting of blue grama, buffalo grass, and Indian ryegrass. It was mature and brown, but offered a good source of protein.

To the west rose the Rocky Mountains, their jagged peaks covered with snow. It was only the end of September, but the higher passes were already filled with the cold, white stuff.

The days were quite comfortable, with abundant sunshine. The nights were cold. The desert climate could not retain the day's warmth.

The cousins rode up into the foothills to hunt and explore. Rod had given them three days off. The aspen trees were bright gold with their trembling leaves. Zac brought a bow and used it to kill a deer. Zac's father had taught all of them to make bows and arrows. Their fathers had taught and stressed the importance of being able to survive in the wilderness. The deer was quickly butchered and the best cuts of meat were wrapped in the skin. Zac slung it to his saddle.

Looking east from the foothills, they could see a brown haze over Denver. It was left from the fires earlier during the summer. The smoke was trapped by the mountains. Their trek continued in the northwest direction, following the Colorado Southern rail tracks.

Toward sunset, they came upon a low log building with a hand-painted sign: "Franklin Trading Post". The men swung down from their horses and took a moment to water them at the trough. Vic rinsed his face while Zac washed the remaining deer blood from his hands and arms.

Leaving the horses at the hitching rail,

they walked into the dimly lit store. A stocky, slightly grayed, middle-aged man stood behind a good old-fashioned wood plank bar. He had a bushy gray moustache, which he had a habit of chewing on.

As their eyes became accustomed to the low light, they saw dusty shelves with various items. Traps hung on the wall. Some furs were tacked to the log walls. The back bar was stocked with rye.

"What would you men like?" the stocky man asked.

Zac had noticed the high cheekbones and brown eyes. The hair that had not turned gray was black.

"I think we would like a round of rye," Dan replied.

"We don't get too many customers up here anymore. When my father quit trapping, he brought me and my mother down here and started the business." He poured three drinks, plus one for himself.

"Some of the old timers still come up to talk about the old days. My mother died years ago, and my father a couple of years ago. I just keep it open for his friends." The stocky bartender raised his glass. "Cheers, gentlemen."

The rye was good. It burned all the way down and warmed the men's stomachs.

Vic set his glass down to be refilled. "I'm Vic August. These other two are Dan and

Zac."

"My pa met a man named August on his way west," the bartender said. "I recall his name was Oli. Mine is Isaac. I was named after my uncle who . . ."

Isaac stopped in mid-sentence as he stared at the open mouths of the three men in front of him.

"You have got to be kidding," Dan blurted out.

"Oli August was our grandfather!" Vic exclaimed.

The next several minutes were a confusion of laughter, exclamations, handshakes, and hugs.

Tom Franklin and his brother Isaac had traveled with their grandfather Oli on his trip west. Tom's brother Isaac was killed by Indians on the Ohio River. When Tom arrived in St. Louis, he'd invited Oli to join him to hunt buffalo or trap beaver. When Oli had declined, Tom had headed for the mountains after acquiring a new Hawken rifle. He had hunted buffalo and trapped for a while.

Along the way, Tom had met an Indian woman and married her. Not wanting to be separated for long periods of time and wanting a better life for the family, they built and ran a trading post.

Vic showed Isaac their grandfather's ledger. He let Isaac read the section about his Uncle Isaac's death.

Vic told Isaac that his grandfather had gone back to the burial site of his Uncle Isaac on the Ohio River and placed a proper marker on the grave.

A tear came to Isaac's eye as he listened to Vic. "As you know, I never met my uncle, and my pa blamed himself for the death of his brother. He had talked his brother into going west. He would be very pleased to know his brother is not lying in an unmarked grave along the river."

The rest of the night was spent sharing conversation and a few more drinks. They built a fire in the fireplace to ward off the evening chill, and roasted venison steaks.

The cousins spent the night sleeping on a pile of furs in the trading post. Their horses were enjoying hay and oats in the lean-to on the side of the log building.

Isaac came back to the trading post at sunrise. Dan and Zac were already up and had a fire going in the fireplace. Vic was curled up in his bedroll, waiting for the room to warm up.

Their mouths were dry and their heads were aching just a bit. Isaac invited them to join him at his house for breakfast.

The house was on the edge of the town of Boulder. It was a two-story house with a wood shingle roof. The boards were weathered, but in good condition.

They stepped into the brightly-lit

dining room. The walls were finished with a gaily printed wall paper. Everything was spotless. They could smell bread baking, mingled with frying bacon. A woman with white hair and green eyes came into the room, carrying fresh-baked bread and a bowl of butter.

Behind her walked a dark-haired girl with hazel eyes carrying a pot of coffee and cups. She had large, red lips and eyes that twinkled. She had on a plain gingham dress that could not hide her stunning figure.

Isaac started the introductions, "This is my wife Caroline and my daughter Eva. These are the men I told you about." He then introduced Dan, Vic, and Zac.

Breakfast consisted of pancakes, eggs, bacon, fresh bread, jam, and honey. This was all washed down with hot, black coffee.

Soon, the men's heads were clear and they were sitting back, full and happy. Dan and Vic noticed that Zac spent a great deal of time watching Eva. She seemed to enjoy his attention.

Before leaving the Franklins, there were promises of coming back. The possibility of doing so was remote. Zac brought the rest of the venison to Caroline. She would can it so it would not go to waste. He spent an extra few minutes talking with Eva before walking back and swinging up onto the piebald.

They waved and rode back down

toward Denver. Eva stood and watched them until they were out of sight.

"I really hope to see them again," Isaac said.

Eva smiled, "I can't speak for Dan and Vic, but Zac you will. He promised to be back in the late spring and asked me to wait."

CHAPTER ELEVEN

On the ride back, their spirits were high. Meeting the Franklins was unbelievable. The stories each had told about Oli August and Tom Franklin traveling west had filled many gaps.

Vic's joy was shattered when he found out that Carla was going east with her father. He knew that they would be parting in Wyoming, but this came too soon.

Carla asked Vic to join her for a last ride along the South Platte River. Vic saddled the buckskin and bay. With the mood depressed, they rode in silence. A few attempts at conversation fell flat. Distracted by the realization that soon they would be apart, they did not notice the three riders pull out on the trail before them.

"It is good to see you again, Mr.

August."

They looked into the smiling face of Eddie Garcia. Behind him sat Cal and Wally.

"We are on a quiet ride, Eddie. We don't want to talk to anyone right now," Vic said as he turned his horse to go around the three.

Eddie side-stepped his horse to block Vic. Vic suddenly realized that he and Carla were in trouble. He stopped his horse, facing the smiling Eddie. Vic knew his loop was on his Colt. His rifle was out of reach in his scabbard.

He looked at Cal and Wally. Their eyes were large and it was evident that they were not comfortable. Vic knew that he had to keep some control of the situation. He dropped his hands, letting his thumbs hang from the sheepskin vest pockets.

He turned his horse, blocking Carla a bit from Eddie, "What do you want, Eddie? You're not holding us up, are you? I haven't been paid yet."

Eddie laughed, "You are not important, Mr. August. We are here for Miss Carla."

Carla wheeled her horse. The split-second Eddie's attention went to her was enough. Vic drew the derringer from the vest pocket and fired at Eddie. Eddie's arm was swinging forward with his whip as Vic shot. The bullet hit the man's shoulder on the side with the whip. It fell harmlessly from his numb hand. He was drawing his Army Colt with the other hand when Vic put his second shot into the center of Eddie's hairy chest.

Eddie managed to get his gun out of his holster and fired a shot, which grazed the side of his own horse. The horse leaped, throwing Eddie to the ground. He lost his gun when he fell and lay on his back, choking on his own blood.

Vic dropped the empty derringer and drew his Colt. He swung the gun on the Ryan brothers. Both sat fixed on their horses with their hands up.

"Don't shoot, Vic!" Cal shouted.

"We didn't know what he was planning to do," Wally pleaded.

Carla pulled up alongside Vic and looked at Eddie breathing his last.

Vic swung down from his horse and walked to Eddie with his Colt in his hand. He looked into the hate-filled eyes of Eduardo Garcia.

"I am not going to offer you the same treatment that you gave the man I wounded in the narrows. I am going to let you die slowly and painfully." Vic holstered the Colt .44.

He tossed Eddie's Army Colt into the river and retrieved his derringer. Vic looked up at the Ryan brothers. "You boys should go back East before you get hurt out here."

He heard Eddie shudder and quit

breathing. "And before you go, bury this useless man. He is littering the road."

Vic swung back onto his bay. Cal rode to catch Eddie's horse. Wally dismounted and dragged Eddie to the side of the road.

Carla and Vic trotted briskly back toward Denver. Suddenly, they had much to say, making promises to write and get back together, and how much they meant to each other.

Before Vic left that night, they stood together under a cottonwood next to her father's rented house. She came into his arms and they kissed. They held each other close, wanting the night to never end.

Vic awoke the next morning, wondering if the promises made were real or the result of meeting Eddie. He felt good about ending Eddie's reign of terror. He hoped that Cal and Wally would go back to Elkader. They weren't cut out for the West.

He was feeling better than he thought he would. He and Carla parted, knowing it was not over. At least in their minds it wasn't.

Dan had gotten the letter he was waiting for the day before. Mary was still determined to come out and meet him in the West. Dan knew that he was not the same man who left Elkader. His fear was that she wouldn't like the man he had become.

There was also a letter from their Grandma Joan. The Alans had broken out of jail and gotten another bullet into Sheriff Wallace. He would be okay after some bed rest. The families were well. She also said that Mary visited her often and missed Dan a lot.

The rest of the letter was about changes around town. Dan wrote a letter back to his Grandma, telling her about meeting Tom Franklin's son. He tried to write one to Mary, but just did not know what to say. He knew Grandma Joan would share her letter with Mary.

Vic missed seeing Carla to the train. It was early morning, and they were starting the herd toward Cheyenne. He heard the train whistle as it pulled out of Denver. It was quite possibly the loneliest sound he had ever heard. He looked back and could see the train moving across the plains.

Fewer men were left driving and watching the herd. Little time was left to think about anything but their work. Vic was glad to be busy. Ling and Pep kept their wagons lumbering on over the rolling plains of brown grass. Dan enjoyed the look of the majestic mountains. Zac was working with the wrangler some days, and others he would ride and scout the trail. He would swing toward the foothills, looking for any landmarks that might match the map.

Cheyenne was a quite modern city for a frontier town. The streets were laid out in equal blocks. Several two and three-story brick buildings lined the streets. The train tracks ran along two sides of the city and included a round house. At night, from a distance, the lights were impressive. The Texans drew their pay and took their horses. Ling and Pep took the wagons into the city and picked up supplies for the remainder of the trip and for the ranch.

The rest of the men kept moving the herd. They were now down to 10 men. Three rode on each flank and three on the drag. Rod rode in front, leading the way. The cattle were trail-broken and gave little trouble driving.

When Ling and Pep returned, they had two additional men with them. The men were from the ranch and on business in Cheyenne. Ling had run into them while leaving town. Every extra hand would be helpful.

One day out of Cheyenne, Zac came back to the herd from scouting. He had two wolf skins. He also had information about their grandfather's valley. During supper they sat off to the side.

"I met two old prospectors," Zac started. "They have been traveling these hills for years. I described the valley our grandfather had spent time in and they were sure they had been there."

"It has a small lake, or pond, on the right side, with a falls. The descriptions were right. That is, except for a small cabin near the pond. Maybe been there 20 years. It was used by hunters."

"How far did they say it was from here?" Vic asked.

"After three days walk west, you will pick up a stream. It flows most of the year. Follow the stream back to the foot hills. Then go south less than a day's walk, and you are at the opening."

Vic opened the ledger and turned to the section on the valley. "Here it is. He met Jed there. He followed the stream on the good horse until he found Jed's body. He buried him under a mound of stones. We just might be able to find that."

With supper over, the men either went on watch or crawled into their bedrolls. The sun would go down early behind the mountains. Most of the leaves were gone from the trees, leaving bare branches reaching toward the sky.

Dan woke to a damp chill. He could feel something brushing his nose and cheeks. Snow! He looked around and the ground was white. Ling was singing next to the fire as he prepared breakfast. The last watch was coming in for their meal. The cattle would not wander far while the men ate.

Vic was excited seeing the large fluffy flakes coming down. Zac was one of the men who came in from the last watch, and his coat and hat was covered with snow. He brushed it off and sat with Dan and Vic.

Ling was making pancakes and had molasses to sweeten them. He had a pan heaped with crisp bacon. There was always plenty of coffee. Every man put down a impressive stack of pancakes. The bacon eaten and coffee drank, they headed for the remuda to get their morning mounts.

Rod told them that they would be driving onto Flying T property by the afternoon. It would be another two-day drive across the ranch before coming to the headquarters. By midday, the snow had melted away and a cold wind blew out of the west.

Vic had his sheepskin vest under his coat. Their chaps helped to cut the wind on their legs. The warmth of the horses they rode gave them some relief. All the men had rabbit skin gloves. Zac liked to wear a woolen poncho rather than a jacket. He liked the freedom to move under it.

A pack of wolves attacked the herd one night while Zac and Dan were on watch. Winchester rifles were pulled and several shots were fired at the pack. There were three confirmed hits, and others were running wounded. It took several hours to drive the scattered cattle back. Daylight found one steer down, hamstrung by the wolves.

Brush was piled onto the steer and a

fire lit. They wanted to leave as little as possible for the remaining wolves. No one wanted to reward their aggressive behavior.

Vic stood watching the fire. He could smell the beef cooking. It was a pleasant smell. He doubted that the fire would do any more than make the beef taste better to them.

It was early afternoon when the herd reached the headquarters. From the rise, the place was very impressive. The buildings were well-laid out, running squarely, north and south or east and west. There were two large barns with corrals. Several outbuildings were used for the blacksmith shop, tool and harness sheds, the cook shack, laundry, washhouse, and sleeping quarters.

The main house sat on a small knoll and was shaded by cottonwood trees. There was a large pasture west of the headquarters that the cattle would be put in for quarantine. Here, each would be checked for diseases or injuries.

Any cattle needing branding would be taken care of. Sorting by age and gender would determine what area of the ranch they would be driven to.

Vic pointed to the stacks of hay in the pasture. Dan nodded and indicated additional stacks east of the headquarters. It was evident that all was ready for the cattle. One of the resident cowboys said there were another 6,000 head spread around the ranch.

The crew was given two days off before starting processing the cattle. The horses were left with the wrangler. With saddles over their shoulders, the men headed for the bunkhouse.

The hoodlum wagon was sitting in front of one bunkhouse. Zac noticed two more bunkhouses that were already occupied. Each bunkhouse had a center door and four windows. The building had twenty bunks and two potbelly stoves for heat. Each stove had a large coffee pot on them. There were five tables for playing cards or writing letters.

Fresh blankets were folded on each bunk. There was a large bin for their dirty blankets. A trunk at the end of each bunk would keep their extra clothes and personal belongings. It could double for a seat.

A shed was built next to each bunkhouse for their saddles, bridles, saddlebags, and horse blankets. There was a series of hitching rails along the front of the bunkhouse. The wrangler would have horses waiting for them each morning, as needed.

It was a very good setup for the average cowboy. The ranch was remote and had to offer extra comfort to keep good hands. It was said most were top hands.

Ling pulled up to the cook shack and had three young Asians busy unloading the chuck wagon. The three boys were his sons, and knew their father's secrets of good chow.

The supper bell clanged and men came from every corner of the ranch, running for the cook shack. The food was served family-style, with heaping bowls of potatoes, loaves of sliced bread, platters of beef steak, and pots of steaming hot beans. The tables had pitchers of water and milk. Desserts consisting of pie or sweet bread would be served with coffee after the main meal.

A well-fed cowboy was a happier and harder-working cowboy. At least that was what the Tilisons figured. Zac noticed that most of the men wore some type of gun, even at supper. Danger was ever present in the North Country. Wolves and rustlers were always on the prowl. The Tilisons wanted their men ready to react.

The next two weeks were dusty, dirty, bone-bruising work. The cattle were brought from the holding pasture, one by one, and checked from head to foot for anything that might cause them to impact the existing cattle. Branding or castrating was done as necessary. Each was checked for parasites or wounds. Once the animal was done, it was put into one of four other pastures. Badly injured or diseased animals were destroyed or separated for slaughter.

Each night, the men limped back to the wash house and cleaned up for supper. Ling and his crew did not disappoint. Each meal was generous and tasty.

A week into the sorting process, Dan sat in front of the bunkhouse smoking a cigarette. He saw Zac and Vic walking toward him.

"Well, we know where we will be spending the winter," Vic informed Dan. "We will be taking 1,000 head to the southwest quarter of the ranch. Rod said there is a line shack fully stocked. We will each have two horses. He will also pay a bonus of $15 for every wolf hide."

Zac sat beside Dan, "We should be able to do some scouting for the gold if the weather permits."

Knowing where they would be spending the winter got them no closer to finding the gold. But they did need a warm place to brave the blizzards and freezing temperatures. The life in a line camp was an isolated one.

Keeping 1,000 head of cattle healthy with wolves, weather, and rustlers trying to take a toll would keep them on their toes.

CHAPTER TWELVE

It was mid-October when the cattle were ready to drive to the line shack. Last minute items were being taken care of. Checking supplies and equipment was a priority. Getting final letters written and leaving next of kin info was taken care of. At the last minute, Rod came out of the main house waving a letter.

"Got a letter for you, Dan. Good thing it came in with today's supplies. Otherwise, you wouldn't have gotten it until spring."

Dan was going to put the letter in his pocket, but changed his mind. Swinging a leg over the saddle horn, he tore open the envelope. It was a letter from Mary.

Dearest Dan,
I read the letter sent to

Grandma Joan. I know you must have a reason you didn't write to me.

I have bad news. Grandma Joan had been feeling poorly for some time. Last week she quietly slipped away. She was very proud of what you and the others are doing. She was especially touched by your meeting with Tom Franklin's son. Your grandpa had often spoken of the Franklins.

Sheriff Wallace was wounded during the Alan's escape. It was three weeks before he was back at work. The Alans headed west and it is expected they will travel all the way to California.

I want you to know I will wait for you. When you are ready I will come west and help you build a home for our family. I often go to the Keystone Bridge and watch the water. It makes me feel closer to you.

RETURN TO OLI'S GOLD

All my Love,
Mary

Dan sat on the horse staring at the mountains. His eyes were burning and his throat ached. He thought back of how tired Grandma Joan was when they last saw her. A fear that he would never see her again became a reality. He wondered if he would ever see any other family members again.

When Zac and Vic rode up, Dan told them about Grandma Joan. The beginning of their trip to the line shack was quiet, with each man left to his own thoughts.

Three other ranch hands helped drive the cattle to the southwest range. The extra three horses were rigged with packs carrying additional items.

Driving the cattle kept their minds off the loss of Grandma Joan. The cattle were not willing to leave the rest of the herd and kept them busy, turning them back toward the range. The ranch hand with the pack animals led the way. He had spent the last winter in the line shack.

As evening came, a light snow started blowing across the plain. The cattle seemed happy to stop and graze. The six men sat around the fire, drinking coffee and eating the biscuits and beef sent by Ling. After the meal, the three ranch hands rode out to check on the herd.

"It is part of the life we have chosen," Zac reflected. "For years, men and women have left home, some traveling across oceans, some over mountains, and like us far to the West. You say good-bye to your family and leave to build a new life, and new family."

"We are lucky," Vic said. "We have each other on this move. Grandpa Oli had no one here in America. He built a family in Elkader."

"It is our responsibility to keep their memories alive. My ancestors told stories around the winter fires, and kept those who had gone before alive in the minds of those who came after," Zac added.

The cousins sat, drinking coffee. A rule taught by their fathers was being broken. They stared into the flames, enjoying the fire's warmth and thinking about the happy hours spent eating cookies with Grandma Joan.

The nights would be spent with two men standing four-hour watches with the cattle and the rest sleeping. There was two inches of snow on the ground when they moved out in the morning. The sky had cleared up and the air was crisp. The mountains were a low, dark ridge on the horizon. The terrain was becoming rougher as they ascended into the foothills.

It was early afternoon when they reached the valley where the cattle would spend the winter. To the north and west, there were natural barriers that would keep them from wandering in those directions. A wide stream ran along the south, which would provide water.

The line shack was built near the stream. A corral was located next to a lean-to on the east side. The line shack was a sturdy, weathered log cabin with two double bunks along opposite walls. A table with four chairs sat between the bunks. A shelf with clothes pegs was on the wall behind the table. The shelf contained books, cards, a checkerboard, and paper and pencils. On the other end of the shack was a lower square stove that would double for cooking and heat.

The floor was made of planks, worn smooth from use. Shelves ran across the wall behind the stove, with dry and canned goods. The south side of the cabin had a plank door and one window. A stack of wood was piled against the wall to the left side of the stove. Additional wood was in a lean-to on the west side of the cabin. Another lean-to on the east side would stable the six horses. Two large stacks of hay were piled near the stable.

Another notable item next to the stable area was the outhouse. The plank walls were not tightly fitted. It promised many a cold morning constitution for the men.

The cattle spread out into the valley to graze, and the three ranch hands got ready to head back, trying to beat the snow. Dan stopped to talk with the tall, lanky hand named Joker. He handed him an envelope and walked back to the cabin. Dan and Vic unpacked the extra horses while Zac rode around the perimeter of the cabin to get the lay of the land.

It was dusk when Zac rode in with a wolf skin. Dan and Vic were sitting at the table with the fire roaring in the stove. A pot of beans bubbled on top and he coffee pot sat near the edge.

Zac put his horse into the stable. He rubbed the piebald down and forked hay into the manger. He liked the racks built for storing the saddles. The Tilisons had an eye for detail.

The smell of beans and coffee were comforting to Zac as he entered the room.

"It smells good enough to be Ling's," he kidded. "I earned us $15 extra pay today. Got a big, old gray one."

The light glowed through the window until late in the evening. The sound of the men talking and laughing reached the sleepy horses. It offered a degree of comfort in their new accommodations.

The men were up early, having slept restlessly in their new bunks. Dan chipped the ice out of the water bucket that was left on the bench outside the door. He used the remaining water to fill the coffee pot. Zac was starting the fire using the Good Knife to cut shavings. Vic burst through the door, shivering and stomping his feet.

"It is freezing out there," he informed them. "You will thank me when you go out there. I put a hover rope in the outhouse. Those boards are cold!"

It was early in the season to have such cold weather. They hoped that it wasn't a sign of things to come. The ground was covered with a thin layer of snow. The cattle were spread across the valley.

By noon, the temperature was just above freezing and Dan turned the horses out into the corral. The daily chores were done. The cousins checked the area around the cabin. The hills north of the shack were covered with aspen. There were clusters of balsam trees scattered on the hill, and the occasional birch tree.

Zac wanted to do some scouting south of the stream. Dan wanted to look north. Vic decided to ride across the valley and check the grazing and locate the haystacks.

"We will meet back here before dark," Vic called out.

Dan rode the chestnut into the aspen. He moved slowly, watching for any sign of movement. He saw some deer tracks and rode in their general direction. He suddenly pulled up the chestnut. Swinging down, he inspected the track in front of him. They were wolf tracks. He surveyed the area and saw several more sets. It was evident they were hunting the deer.

He glanced back toward the valley and could see the grazing cattle at the far side. It appeared that the wolves had not discovered the cattle. He estimated that there were up to a dozen in this pack.

Vic was pleased with the amount of grass he found. It stood about knee high and would be available well into the snow season. He found two dozen haystacks strategically placed around the upper valley. The lower valley ran ten miles east. He found a few deer tracks and some rabbit tracks.

Zac crossed the knee-deep stream. It was fast flowing, and should resist freezing over until well into the depths of winter. He let the piebald have its head and it walked swiftly toward the south. It felt good to ride without cattle to push.

He stopped on a rise and slowly scanned the plains in front of him. He could see a dark line of tracks cutting through the thin snow about a mile below. Zac watched for any movement. After he was satisfied, he urged the piebald toward the tracks.

They were made by a mix of two dozen shod and unshod horses. Zac could not make out any sign of travois' being pulled. Zac determined that they were a hunting party. The braves may have strayed from the reservation, more than likely hunting elk in the foothills.

Zac followed the tracks for a couple of miles. He found an area where they stopped to look over the cattle in the valley. Two of the horsemen had ridden toward the valley and stood for a while, then turned, rejoined the others and continued south.

He realized that the hunters knew that the cattle were in the valley. Zac was guessing that they were Cheyenne or Lakota. The Indian agency was well-known for shorting the reservation tribe's food rations. With food being scarce, the cattle would be easy game. He decided that he would keep an eye on this area.

The cousins arrived back at the line shack within an hour of each other. Dan had a deer slung across the back of his saddle. Vic was getting the fire going, and Zac was watering the riding stock. Dan hung the deer on the side of the line shack and took his horse down to the stream.

"I saw some pony tracks of a hunting party," Zac let Dan know.

"I saw a large pack of wolf tracks," Dan said. "Could be part of the pack you got one from."

In the following days, scouting the area created a picture of problem spots that would need watching. This time of year, rustlers should not be a big issue. Wolves would be a bigger problem.

By late November, the men had fallen into a routine. The heavy snow had held off. They had shot five more wolves.

One evening, Vic had meat roasting over an outdoor fire as Dan and Zac came back from checking the herd. The strips of meat were nicely browned and dripped juice on the hot coals.

"Over here," he called. "Broiled meat for hungry men."

They stood, chewing the stringy meat.

"What is it, Vic?" Dan asked.

Zac chewed the meat, smiling from ear to ear. "You don't know what it is, Dan?"

"It is prime wolf," Vic informed Dan.

Dan's jaw dropped, and he turned and spit the meat out. "What in the world are you cooking wolf for?"

"I was reading grandpa's ledger," he said. "I got to the part where when he turned the tables on the wolves. He made them his meal instead of the other way around."

Dan looked at Zac and Vic chewing the meat. "What is good for grandpa should be good for us."

He gingerly picked another strip of meat and slowly chewed. "You know what? Grandpa knew how to eat well."

Laughing, the cousins finished the meat and headed into the cabin for coffee.

The howling of the wind gradually

woke Vic. The air in the cabin was unusually cold, and he burrowed his head deeper in the covers. The door was rattling on its metal hinges. A gust blew down the stove pipe and shook the stove lids.

Vic leaped from his top bunk and stumbled, looking for the lantern. With shaking hands, he raised the glass and struck a match. The floor had a slippery, cold feeling. The flame caught the wick and Vic set the lantern on the table.

He stared at the table in surprise. It was covered with a thin layer of snow. He stepped back, looking. The entire cabin was the same. The howling wind was forcing snow through every accessible crack in the cabin and depositing it everywhere.

Zac had chosen the other top bunk, and Dan had the lower bunk below him. As Vic expected, their blankets were also covered. Both Dan and Zac had their heads under covers. Vic had no idea of what time it was. Even if the sun was up, the blowing snow outside would block it out.

With the occasional gust coming down the stove pipe, Vic had a difficult time lighting it. Finally, the fire caught. A generous amount of smoke blew into the room.

Zac threw off his covers, coughing from the smoke. "Did you light the cabin on fire also?"

"Grab a broom and sweep the snow off

the floor," Vic shouted over the storm. "I got the fire going and will go check on the stock."

Pulling on his sheepskin coat, a woolen hat, and rabbit skin mittens he had just made, Vic stepped out the door. The wind almost pushed him back into the cabin as he fought to close the door behind him. His breath was torn away as he faced the storm. He could not open his eyes.

Vic turned back to the cabin wall and sheltered his face. In preparation for these type of storms, ropes had been strung from the cabin door to the stable, woodshed, and outhouse. He groped around until he found the rope that led to the stable. With his eyes closed tight, little by little, he worked his way along the rope. The wind was frigid and tearing at his clothes.

He bumped into the wall of the stable. He felt around with numb, mittened hands for the door handle. The door closure was an oval flat grip on the outside. It was whittled down to a round peg that fit through a hole bored beside the door. A foot-long rectangular piece was fitted to the inside part of the peg and would keep the door closed when turned.

Vic found the flat grip and turned it a quarter-turn. The stable door burst open, pulling him inside. The horses were startled as he rushed in, stomping and kicking their stalls. Pushing the door shut, Vic turned the closure.

It took just a moment to light the lantern. The warmth of the horses in the small stable felt wonderful. Vic put his arms around the bay and absorbed the horse's heat.

Like the cabin, the stable had snow blowing in from every crack. The room was fog-filled from the warm breath of the horses mixing with the frigid air from outside.

There was hay stored in a loft above the stable, to be fed during storms. A barrel of water was kept in the corner for use in the cabin or watering the horses. The heat of the stock prevented the water from freezing.

Vic pitched hay to the horses and gave each of them a bucket of water. Finishing, he blew the lantern out and stepped back into the storm. While the snow was still blinding, Vic could now tell that it was daylight. He needed to use the outhouse. He stood at the stable door, being pummeled by wind-driven snow.

The thought of working his way back to the cabin door and then taking another rope to the outhouse did not make sense. He knew that the outhouse was just 30 feet behind the cabin. Vic felt his way along the stable wall until he reached the far corner. He knew that the outhouse was straight off the corner.

Vic got his bearings the best he could and stepped away from the stable, cutting on an angle just to the left of the outhouse. He held his arm up to catch the rope. The snow was a foot and a half deep. Suddenly, Vic's foot caught on something and he tumbled headlong into the snow.

Vic got to his hands and knees and opened his eyes to see where he was. The snow forced him to close them and duck his head into the crook of his arm. He realized he had lost one of his mittens. He stumbled back to his feet, his eyes closed tight and tucked the bare hand into his coat. A wave of fear swept over Vic. He did not know which way he was facing!

Vic tried to remember which way the wind was blowing before he fell, and he did not know for sure. Standing in the storm with his eyes closed, Vic could feel the cold creeping through his clothes.

"Can anyone hear me!" he shouted. All he heard in return was the howling wind.

Vic knew he'd tripped over a drift. He turned ninety degrees at a time and felt with his mittened hand for the drift or his tracks. On the third turn, Vic fell again. Panic was building. He could not tell up from down. His face and hands were numb. He had heard stories of people freezing to death a few feet from their door.

He knew he could not see and had absolutely no idea which way the stable, cabin, or outhouse were. He knew he could not walk with his arms up, looking for one of the ropes. Vic pulled the woolen cap down over his face.

"Don't be a fool and panic," he mumbled. "Warmth and shelter is just few feet away."

Again, he shouted, "Can you hear me!"

In the howling wind, he could barely hear his own voice. Vic felt his body begin to shake. He knew he had only minutes to find one of the buildings or die of hypothermia.

He refused to let this storm get the best of him. Vic sunk to his knees and forced himself to rethink everything since he came out of the cabin. Wind direction might be his only asset.

When he stepped out of the cabin the wind blew the door open. When he turned to face the cabin the wind was at his back. He knew that wind direction was the key to finding his way back to shelter.

He suddenly realized that he couldn't remember where he was when he'd let go of the building. He mind was not working.

"I must remember!"

His mouth was filled with blowing snow, and he began to cough.

Drawing from every bit of his conscious will to survive, he chose a direction. He tried to stand and found his legs would not support him. Something hit him and everything went black.

Vic felt warm. The storm seemed further away. He knew as his body would start to shut down he would feel warm again. He did not fear what was coming, but rather welcomed it.

He heard a clang of metal on metal. He tried to open his eyes, but could not. He tried to sit up but something was stopping him.

"He's waking up, Zac."

It was Dan's voice!

Was Dan in heaven too? How did Dan die?

"Hey Vic, good to see you are still with us," Zac said as he knelt near the bunk where Vic lay.

"Your eyes are damaged from the snow. You won't be able to see for a while," Dan said as he placed a damp cloth over Vic's eyes.

Zac pulled a chair over to the bunk Vic lay on. "Dan went out to look for you. He saw you had finished watering and feeding the horses. He then went to the rope for the outhouse. As he was working his way along the rope, he bumped into you."

"He grabbed your coat with one hand and held on to the rope with the other. He dragged you back to the cabin. Your eyes were wide open under the cap. They were red and swollen.

"We think you were staring at the snow for a while. With luck, you will be able to see again in the next day or so."

Dan set a cup of beef broth down on the table. He propped Vic up and handed him the warm cup. "Here, drink this. It will warm your insides."

"You were lucky, Vic," Dan continued. "You fell under the outhouse rope. If you had been a couple of feet either way, I wouldn't have tripped over you. You have a little bit of frost bite on your cheeks and one hand. Other than that, you came through okay."

Dan walked back to the stove. He added some potatoes and more beef to the boiling pot of broth. He wished that they could get a doctor to check Vic's eyes. If Vic had stared into the snow and frozen the surfaces of his eyes, he might be permanently blind. If he had opened them and had hard flakes of snow hit them and cause scratches, then his blindness would be temporary.

Zac poured Vic a cup of coffee and stirred honey into it. Vic took the cup and smiled as he took sips of the sweet brew.

His throat was feeling better. "It was my own stupid fault. I tried a shortcut to the outhouse and got lost."

"We are all allowed a few mistakes," Dan called over. "You just like to make big ones."

By the next day, Vic was able to see. His eyes were irritated and they continued putting the damp cloths on them.

The storm lasted two more days. The snow outside was only about 12 inches deep. There were drifts much higher behind the structures.

They were unable to see any of the cattle. Zac took the piebald and went to look for them. Dan led the horses to water and refilled the water barrels and replaced the hay in the loft. He spent an hour splitting wood, then stacked some near the front door and replaced the wood near the stove.

Vic sat at the table, resting his eyes. Slowly, the realization of how close he'd come to freezing to death began to sink in. Zac and Dan kept the issue light, which Vic appreciated. He knew each man was responsible for minimizing risks when they were so far from any type of help. He had already given himself a good scolding for taking the shortcut.

Zac found the cattle, bunched downwind three miles away. Overall, they seemed to have come through the blizzard okay. He started them back toward their main grazing area.

The cousins spent their winter hours doing daily chores, checking on the cattle, hunting wolves, and hunkering down during storms. Books were read and reread until they could almost recite them word for word.

Notes written by Grandpa Oli in the ledger were studied. They worked out a time frame for the distance traveled from the green valley he had recovered in. It would be the first place to strike out for.

RETURN TO OLI'S GOLD

One cold February day, a trapper named Billy stopped by the cabin. Fire had burnt his winter quarters and he was heading for Cheyenne to spend the rest of the season. He stayed almost a week. The men talked with him by the hour, asking questions about the mountains and foothills.

He had wintered one year on the Big Horn River. Billy said the area was plum full of valleys and box canyons. He mentioned the rumor that there was Spanish gold hidden in the area, but he did not believe the Spanish had ever gotten that far north.

One morning, Billy had his packs bundled and announced that it was time to head for Cheyenne. Billy was given a haunch of venison and a couple of dozen biscuits. In return, he gave them two wolf skins. Vic had entered everything Billy said about the Big Horn River on a blank page in the ledger.

It was mid-March and the cousins were tired of the snow. Dan awoke early. He started a fire in the stove and went to the door to go to the outhouse. He opened the door and was greeted with a gust of warm air. He could hear melting snow dripping from the eaves. The sun was just coming up in the east.

They knew that there was another month of misery weather left, but the warmer air was a spirit-lifting change. It was three more weeks before any serious melting of the snow began.

CHAPTER THIRTEEN

The snow melted quickly and the stream soon was running over its banks. The water ran within 50 feet of the cabin. The daily cleaning of the stable left stacks of manure that replaced the haystacks that were there when the men had arrived.

The cattle were thin, but fit. Their rough winter coats were beginning to shed. Some of the sunnier hills had some green grass that was quickly discovered by the cattle.

Zac and Vic went to scout the foothills to see if any of the landmarks matched those in the ledger. Dan rode into the valley to check on the cattle.

Dan had ridden five miles east when he came across the tracks of 30 to 40 cattle. By the way the tracks ran, he could tell that they were being driven. A closer inspection told him that the tracks were a day old.

Bit by bit, Dan walked across the trampled earth, looking for horse tracks. He found the tracks of three horses. He was relieved to see they were all shod. He remembered the tracks that were found last fall. He didn't want to have to face a party of Cheyenne braves.

Dan looked toward the foothills. Zac and Vic would not be back until dark. If he waited for them to join him, the cattle rustlers would have a two-day start.

Dan was riding one of the extra horses. He rode it hard back to the cabin. He walked it the last quarter-mile to let it cool down. After switching his saddle to the chestnut, he rubbed the ridden horse down and put it in the corral and forked in some hay. He left a note on the table telling Zac and Vic where he was going.

With extra rations and his bedroll tied to the back of his saddle, and extra cartridges in his saddlebags, Dan moved out at an intercepting angle to cut the trail of the stolen cattle. He wore Vic's sheepskin vest under his buckskin jacket to ward off the chill that morning.

It was noon when Dan cut the tracks. They were driving the cattle in the direction of Denver. Dan was confident that he could catch up to the cattle by noon the next day.

He wasn't sure what he would do when he caught up to them. What he did know was that when it was over, the rustlers would no longer have the cattle.

Dan stopped for the night, well after dark. The night was cold and there would be frost. He rubbed the chestnut down and picketed it on a patch of grass. After a quick meal of biscuits and coffee, Dan rolled up in his blankets.

The eastern sky was just getting light when he awoke. It was cold. It had been some time since Dan had slept on the ground. He woke up a little stiff. After a quick cup of hot coffee and some beef jerky, Dan kicked dirt over the fire. With the chestnut saddled and his gear stowed, Dan continued to follow the cattle.

He heard them before he saw them. Dan knew that when he went over the next rise he would see the rustlers. Just south of the rise, Dan saw where water had cut through the rise. He rode through the cut and was soon ahead of the cattle.

He could see the rustlers lazily pushing the cattle. One on each flank and one riding drag. Using the spyglass given to him by Rod Tilison, he looked the rustlers over. There were two older men and one that looked about seventeen.

All were armed with handguns. One had a rifle in his scabbard. As he watched the cattle coming toward him, Dan failed to hear the horseman come up behind him.

"You like my cattle, mister?" Dan heard a voice say behind him.

Dan slowly turned the chestnut around to look at the speaker. Sitting on a crow-bait horse was a bearded old man with a tattered coat and hat. He had a jagged tooth in the front of his mouth, with the rest missing. In his hand he held an Army Colt that was anything but tattered.

Dan realized that he had just met a fourth rustler who was waiting for the other three. He was older than the others, and by the way he held himself Dan figured that he was the leader.

"If I were you, I would drop your weapons in the dirt and move away from them," the old man instructed him.

Dan knew he wasn't going to let this man take him prisoner. Once disarmed, he was sure that the man would kill him.

"My name is Dan August. Those cattle belong to The Flying T ranch. I'm responsible for protecting the cattle. I will give you a chance to ride away and we can forget this ever happened," Dan reasoned.

"Drop your guns or I will blow you out of the saddle," he growled.

Dan carefully pulled the Winchester and dropped it, and then removed the loop from his Colt .44 and dropped it.

"You think I'm stupid? The knife also," the old man snapped.

Dan pushed his jacket back and pulled the knife from its sheath. As he did so, he slipped his hand into the vest pocket. He could feel the cold gun lying at the bottom. His hand closed around Vic's derringer.

As the old man watched the knife fall, Dan withdrew his hand and shot him in the forehead with the sneak gun. The old man's mouth dropped open and confusion crossed his face as he slumped over and fell from the saddle.

Quickly dismounting, Dan scooped up his weapons. An inspection told him that they were free from dirt. He could see that the three other rustlers had stopped and were looking in the direction of the shot.

Dan led the old man's horse into some trees and tied it. He mounted the chestnut and rode to the edge of the cut where the others could see him.

"You have stolen Flying T cattle. I want you to drop your guns and move away from the cattle!" he shouted.

The three men spurred their horses and rode for cover. An unexplained rifle shot knocked the man on the right flank off his horse. Dan swung his Winchester and lined up on the man on the left flank. He squeezed off a quick shot. The man twisted in the saddle and fell to the ground. The young man riding drag stopped and raised his hands.

Dan rode out carrying his rifle, searching for the other shooter. He saw the piebald with Zac come up on the rise. Waving, Dan went to check on the man he had shot at. Vic appeared over the rise and went to cover the young man riding drag.

Zac's bullet killed the rustler on the right flank. Dan's shot hit the man high in the shoulder. He was stunned from the fall from his horse. Dan relieved him of his gun and helped him to his feet.

As it turned out, none of the men were related. The old man had scouted the valley and then found these three men to rustle the cattle. The young man's name was Roy Hobbs. The wounded man was Rolli Smith. The young man dug graves for the unnamed dead rustlers.

There was a small railroad town named Medicine Bow, 40 miles west of them. It had a sheriff, so the men decided that Vic could push the cattle back toward the valley, and Zac and Dan would bring the rustlers to the sheriff.

The stay in Medicine Bow was short. Zac and Dan rode back toward the valley after leaving Roy and Rolli with the sheriff. Dan felt a bit sorry for the rustlers. The sheriff told them they should have just hung them and saved the town the cost of a trial. Both gave the sheriff their depositions and left.

There was no doubt justice would be swift and severe.

When they arrived back at the cabin, they found that the two ranch hands had returned to help drive the cattle back onto the home range.

The cousins spent a week at the main ranch, catching up on news and readying their gear for an extended stay in the foothills. Ling had made them a pack of beef and biscuit sandwiches to take with them. They were sitting in front of the bunkhouse, waiting for their final pay.

Vic sat reading the letter from Carla. He had already read it a dozen times, but he liked the warm feeling it gave him inside. Dan had no mail waiting for him. He sat leaning back in his chair, studying the end of his cigarette.

Zac appeared to be sleeping, enjoying the sun. He had started to grow his hair longer, and it was now shoulder-length. His left eye opened as Rod walked out of the headquarters.

"I got your pay here, along with your wolf skin money," Rod said, handing each their winter wages. "There is also a little extra for saving the cattle from the rustlers. Your herd fared the best of all of them over the winter."

"Two of the other herds had some rustling. No doubt the same fellows you ran into. The trails were too old to follow by the time it was noticed."

Rod pulled out a cigar and bit the tip off and lit it slowly with a wooden match. Once the cigar was drawing nicely, he motioned the men to sit for a minute.

"I imagine you are heading out to look for the gold your grandfather found."

While they fought not to show any signs of surprise, they were sure that they did not do a good job of it.

"Don't worry, I got all I can handle here without going and chasing gold," Rod smiled. "Jacob Wolfe told me about the gold and how your grandfather came back with Spanish coins. He figured you men wanted to drive the herd into the West to be close to the gold and then search for it."

"We had an old trapper named Billy come through last winter and talk of a gold rumor," Dan replied coolly. "There are many rumors about lost gold. We don't pay much mind to them."

Rod stood up and grinned at the men. "I am sure you don't." Reaching out to shake their hands, he wished them good hunting.

Each had a nice bundle of money from the winter's work. Rod had given them an extra month's pay as a bonus. They left the Flying T ranch with three riding horses and two pack horses. The direction they struck out for was Cheyenne.

CHAPTER FOURTEEN

Cheyenne was bustling. Steam trains were bringing goods in and taking local products out. Large wagons hauled the freight away from the depot to points near and far. Buggies were constantly moving along the streets.

The plains were covered with spring flowers and tender grasses. Fruit trees and berry bushes were covered with blossoms. The cousins pulled up outside of town and looked in awe at the city. They felt poorly dressed compared to the people they saw.

The cousins rode into the city and headed for a livery stable. Zac led the way into the wide doorway and swung down. The smell of hay, oats, and leather surrounded them.

"Can I help you gents?" an old fellow

with bushy eyebrows and shaggy graying hair asked.

He stepped out of the shadows, and you could have knocked the cousins over with a feather. It was Carlos from St. Paul!

Vic stepped forward with an outstretched hand. "Carlos, great to see you. Is Huck here with you?"

The look on Carlos' face told them that the news about Huck was not good. "My good friend Huck died in his sleep last fall. I couldn't stay at the train depot without him, and left right after the funeral. Ended up in Cheyenne and took the job at this livery."

The sadness that Huck was gone was short-lived. The excitement of finding a familiar face outweighed it.

The horses were quickly unsaddled and rubbed down. Soon, they were enjoying a generous share of oats in nice, clean stalls. Carlos had a pot of coffee on and invited the three to join him.

The cousins sat with Carlos in the office that doubled as his bedroom, and sipped the strong hot brew. Carlos cocked his head and looked at Zac.

"You're letting it grow long," he commented about his hair.

Zac sipped his coffee and nodded.

"Looks good on you."

Carlos recommended a hotel to stay at. He also told them of a café where they could get a good meal and a fair price. He let them leave their extra gear in the back of the office. Carlos recommended leaving their guns with him.

"Local law don't take kindly to gun-toting cowboys."

Carlos put the guns with their gear. Vic kept his derringer in the vest pocket. They all kept their knives.

After handshakes and promises to visit more, the cousins left the livery stable with Vic in the lead. The hotel was five blocks up the street. Dan pointed to a horse-drawn trolley car and the three jumped on.

After checking into a room and leaving their saddlebags, it was time to cross the street and try Lem's Café. The tables were covered with red and white-checkered table cloths. The dining room was clean and cheerful looking. A pretty redhead with freckles was waiting on tables.

"The specials are on the board over there. I would recommend the shepherd's pie," she cooed. "It's made with beef, not lamb. Lem brought the recipe over from England."

"Does he make a good cup of tea?" Zac asked.

"He sure does," she replied, pushing her bosom forward just a bit.

Zac blushed. "I'll have the shepherd's pie, and tea to drink."

Smiling broadly, Vic and Dan ordered

the same.

Three plates loaded with the potato-covered pie were served, along with a loaf of bread cut into thick slices. There was a small bowl with fresh-churned butter.

Filled with the tasty shepherd's pie and bread, the cousins sat and sipped their tea. They were drinking it English-style, with milk.

The pretty redhead leaned forward, removing the empty plates from the table.

"I like to watch hungry men enjoy their meal. We have two types of pies for dessert. Wild strawberry with rhubarb, or custard," she teased, and her hip brushed against Dan on the way to the kitchen.

"I'll have some of that strawberry rhubarb," Vic called as she disappeared into the kitchen.

Walking out of the café, all were rubbing their bellies, now over-filled with the meal plus the pie. They debated back and forth whether tea or coffee was better with a meal. While the tea was a pleasant change, Dan missed his evening coffee.

The sun had gone down while they'd eaten. Dan was glad to put a little distance between the redhead and them. She just might be too much to handle. The sound of a piano drew the cousins toward the Cheyenne Saloon. The front was lit, and they could hear the sound of poker chips and ladies' laughter.

There was an impressive mahogany bar along the right side of the room. The back bar was lined with mirrors and bottles of every type of drink one could imagine. Four large chandeliers lit the large room. Card games were being played on the left side, and a few empty tables were in the middle of the room for drinking customers.

The three decided to stand at the bar and have a drink. Walking to the back part of the saloon, they stood with the wall protecting one side. While there might not be the need, a little caution in a strange town was always a good idea.

The three ordered rye whiskey. The burly bartender hesitated a minute, looking at Zac, and then decided to get their drinks.

"I think they're still fighting the Indian wars here," Vic whispered.

The three toasted the redheaded waitress and tossed down the rye, then set their glasses down for another refill.

"I'm not supposed to serve no Injuns," the bartender grumbled.

"You're in luck, my friend," Vic said glibly. "Zac here is of Finnish origin."

Shaking his head and still grumbling, the bartender left the bottle and moved down to serve other customers.

Vic elbowed Dan and pointed to the poker table in the far corner. Dan looked over and couldn't see what Vic was looking at.

Zac looked over and let out a slow breath. "I believe you have just pointed out Sid Alan."

Dan glanced and turned back to Vic and Zac. "I think you are right. I wonder if Len is around?"

Finishing their drinks, Vic tossed some coins onto the bar to cover them. Sid looked up and gave them a long, hard look. Walking out of the saloon toward the hotel, Zac noticed a man smoking down the street. He was using his left arm and seemed to favor his right arm.

The next morning was bright and sunny. The three were eating an excellent breakfast at the café. The redhead was not at work. Vic asked a surly middle-aged woman about her.

"Too damn lazy to work mornings," she snarled.

In spite of the less than pleasant lady serving them, they enjoyed their morning meal. It was served with plenty of hot coffee.

The three stopped in front of the café and Dan rolled a cigarette. He bent down to light the smoke when a bullet parted the back of his hair. The report of the gunshot was loud in the morning air. Dan hit the ground, stunned. Vic pulled the derringer as he and Zac took cover around the corner of the café.

Vic heard running steps behind the buildings across the street. He didn't see the shooter, and wasn't even sure which alley the shot had come from. Zac stepped out to help Dan to his feet.

The sheriff came running up the street. "Drop the gun there, young man," he said in a commanding voice.

Vic looked at the sheriff holding a gun on him. He was a short, stocky man with a thick blond moustache.

Vic stepped out and placed the gun on the ground. "We were shot at, I didn't shoot at anyone."

Vic joined Zac and Dan. The sheriff gave a disapproving look at the three men.

"You cowboys come into Cheyenne and think you can take over the town!" the sheriff snapped.

Vic fought to control his anger, "I appreciate how you feel about cowboys, but we were minding our own business and just finished breakfast. We're sure the shooter was one of the Alan brothers. Sid saw us last night. We brought them in for bank robbery back in Iowa."

"That may be so, but they ain't wanted in Wyoming. I want you three out of town today. If you and the Alans want to kill each other, do it out on the plains."

There was no reasoning with the sheriff. He had put his gun away and picked up the derringer.

"We will pick up some supplies this morning and be out of your town by noon," Vic said evenly. "I'll want the derringer back."

"Pick it up on the way out of town," the sheriff replied, and with that he turned and walked back to his office.

The three crossed the street to their hotel watching every corner. Zac checked Dan's scalp.

"You were lucky, Dan. It barely drew blood."

Zac cleaned the wound with a cloth near the wash basin. It was time to check out of the hotel. With saddlebags slung over their shoulders, they headed for the livery stable. Carlos was told what had happened and about the sheriff.

"Sheriff Kent, he is a tough one. Trouble is, he don't know you men or the Alans. He is paid to keep the town quiet. The way he looks at it is you men will bring noise to town. With you gone, the noise goes away." Shaking his head, Carlos continued. "It ain't right, but he has all the cards on his side."

Vic and Zac went to buy the needed supplies while Dan went to the telegraph office. He sent a telegram to Sheriff Wallace in Elkader, saying that the Alans were spotted in Cheyenne.

Dan then wrote a short letter to Mary, telling her they were heading for the foothills to look for ranch land. He mentioned the trouble with Sheriff Kent in Cheyenne and figured the word would get to Sheriff Wallace.

He was careful not to give her any hope of coming west. He doubted that she would like the man he had become.

Carlos told them that the Alan brothers had left Cheyenne shortly after taking the shot at them. He had gotten word from the livery on the other side of town.

The cousins decided to leave Cheyenne toward the east, then circle north and finally head west to look for the green valley. The plain was wide open, and from a rise of 100 feet someone watching for movement could see almost 10 miles on a clear day. The rolling plain offered cover in the dips, but at some point you have to go over a rise and could be seen.

They rode three hours south before setting up a quick camp to make supper. The fire was kept small and allowed to burn out after eating. A full coffee pot was left near the remaining coals for later. The plan was to rest until sunset.

As the lonely howls of the wolves and coyotes split the night, while foxes hunted for mice, and the crickets chirped, three silent figures moved through the night leading two pack horses. The lukewarm coffee helped them stay awake.

It was near daybreak before the next camp was chosen. It was on a stream 30 miles northeast of Cheyenne, near a grove of oak trees with budding leaves. The horses were rubbed down and picketed on good grass. After drinking a little water to wash down some jerky, bedrolls were spread out and the cousins went right to sleep.

Vic woke up at noon. He felt for his Winchester and Colt. Both were where he had left them. The sun was warm and the sky had puffy clouds scattered across it. Zac's bedroll was empty. Dan was beginning to stir.

Vic got up and put together a small fire. Wood from the oaks was plentiful, with several large and small branches lying beneath them, undoubtedly snapped of by wet snow or freezing rain during the winter.

Dan was up rolling his blankets while Vic finished adding coffee to the boiling water. Zac came back with six fat trout.

"I would have been back sooner, but the last trout wouldn't cooperate and let me catch it."

Zac was in a good mood. He was happiest away from towns. He now wore his hair in a loose braid like his father.

"You clean them, Zac, and I'll cook them," Vic offered.

"I am not going to let you ruin some perfectly good fish," Zac scoffed. "I will clean and cook them."

It wasn't long before they were enjoying broiled fish, biscuits and jam, and strong hot coffee.

"We're not far from where I met the two

miners," Zac informed the others.

They could see the mountains low on the western horizon. Zac drew a map with a stick in the dust.

"The stream we are on turns to the south about a mile west of here. We need to travel west looking for a stream flowing northeast. We follow it for two days and that will bring us within a half day's ride of grandpa's green valley."

Vic and Dan looked at the crude map in the dust. They quickly committed it to memory and brushed over the map.

Vic sat back and took a gulp of his coffee. "We will then go north until we reach the Stinking Water River."

It appeared that they had evaded the Alan brothers. Zac spent time watching the back trail and found nobody was tracking them. On the third day, the stream was reached that appeared to be the one where their grandpa had tracked Jed.

While they sat and ate their evening meal, Zac suddenly stood up and slipped into the brush. Vic and Dan could see four riders coming toward them from the north. Their guess was that the riders were Cheyenne off the reservation.

The hackamores on their ponies were decorated with feathers. The riders were stripped to the waist and wore deerskin pants. Their rifles were older single-shot.

Their headbands held shoulder-length black hair off their faces.

The Cheyenne stopped a distance from the camp and sat staring at Dan and Vic. Dan had his rifle cradled across his lap and acted like he was cleaning it. Vic had his rifle leaning on a stump within easy reach.

The large brave in the center, who appeared to be the leader began to sign. He moved his hand flat and away from his chin. Dan and Vic stared, wondering what it meant. Zac had moved around and got the piebald. He rode out to meet the Cheyenne, sitting tall and square on the horse.

Zac stopped short of the Cheyenne and began to communicate with them in sign language. After a short time, Zac rode back to the camp while the braves watched him. He picked up a haunch of venison hanging on a nearby tree.

Zac returned to the Cheyenne and handed them the venison. The leader took the meat, and after a few more motions turned and rode east. Zac swung down from the piebald and led it back to the camp.

"What was that all about?" Dan asked.

"The Cheyenne are hunting for game and asked if we had seen any. I told them we had seen little. I told them we had extra meat and would be happy to share. By giving them food, we show that we respect them. We offered it as an equal. He thanked us and said in the future they would give us some elk."

The men knew that the conflict between the tribes and the white man had ended 10 years before. But just like there were white men traveling the west looking for opportunities, there were also Indians looking for easy marks.

Dan was getting the pack horses ready when he made a recommendation. "We are about to head into rough country while we search. We left Cheyenne without getting all the items we should have, due to the sheriff. Medicine Bow is just north of us. We should finish stocking up there."

Vic chuckled. "You noticed we still need a shovel and pick, didn't you?"

Dan grinned. "Yup."

When they entered Medicine Bow, it was almost mid-day. The first man they recognized was Sheriff Chick Arnold.

He gave a hard look at Vic and then turned to Dan and Zac. "You wouldn't happen to have them robbers with you?"

"It is good to see you again, sheriff. No, we don't. Didn't know there were any robbers to be got," Dan replied.

"They bought some stuff from Percy's Mercantile, then shot him and emptied his register," he snorted. "Old Percy didn't die right off. He gave a pretty good description of the two, right down to the one with the bad right arm."

"Bad right arm?" Dan inquired.

He then described the Alan brothers to the sheriff.

"So you have seen them," the sheriff exclaimed.

Dan brought the sheriff up to date with their history with the Alan brothers, including the shot they took at him in Cheyenne.

"If you find 'em, kill 'em, and bring in their heads," Sheriff Chick said. "We got a $300 reward for the one who does."

The cousins pulled up in front of the mercantile. Tying the horses at the hitching rail, Dan stepped up on the walk and rolled a cigarette. Zac and Vic tied the pack horses and then joined Dan. The Percy widow was working behind the counter.

Mrs. Percy was drawn and tired. She looked up as the three men walked in. For a moment, fear showed in her eyes.

Vic stepped forward. "Mrs. Percy, the sheriff told us about your husband. We would like to extend our condolences. We once brought in the Alans, the men who did it. If we ever see them again, they will pay for what they did to you."

Mrs. Percy smiled, and tears began to run down her cheeks. "I'm sorry boys, I thought that I was cried out."

Blowing her nose loudly, she then dabbed her eyes and took a deep breath.

"What can I help you with?"

Soon, the needed pick and shovel were purchased, along with some dynamite. They wanted to be ready for anything. After adding a few comfort items to the order, everything was secured on the pack horses.

"While you and Dan were looking for dynamite and caps, I talked a bit more with Mrs. Percy about the robbery," Vic told Zac. "The posse tracked them to the foothills ten miles west. The trail was lost. After a day of looking for it, they gave up and came back."

Zac looked at Vic. "We don't want to go traipsing across country looking for the Alans, who have a week's start on us."

"It's not right that that those who killed her husband, and stole their money, are out there living it up."

"Who's living it up?" Dan asked, walking up to Vic and Zac.

Zac told Dan about Vic's ridiculous idea.

"We would need to leave the pack horses with someone," Dan concluded.

Zac furled his brow, "You're not thinking about doing it, are you?"

"We got the whole summer to find the gold."

Sheriff Arnold made arrangements with the livery to keep the horses on the town's tab. He then sketched a map of the chase and where the trail had been lost.

Zac was still muttering when they left Medicine Bow. Vic knew Zac was just giving him a hard time and was more than willing to help bring the Alans to justice.

The cousins arrived at the foothills an hour before dusk. Dan and Vic set up camp while Zac rode out to look for any sign. It was an hour after dark when Zac returned.

Vic was frying bacon over the fire and had a pot of coffee on the edge. He set the fry pan onto a flat rock and dug out a paper parcel holding a half loaf of sourdough bread.

The three sat around the frying pan, spearing strips of bacon with their knives and dipping slices of bread into the grease. The coffee was good and strong. It tasted mighty fine on the cool May evening.

"The area is sure messed up with all the riding back and forth," Zac said. "If the Alans had hired them to cover their trail, they couldn't have done a better job."

"So you couldn't find anything?" Dan inquired.

"I didn't say that," Zac smiled. "There was a water hole in the rocks where the Alans stopped to water the horses. The posse didn't find it. There is a long granite ridge that leads down into a valley. I found faint markings of the horses' hooves heading that way. The posse hadn't wiped them out."

"Once in the valley, there doesn't appear to be a way out for some distance. The posse did not go into the valley. There hasn't been rain since the robbery. We should be able to pick up the trail in the morning."

All three were up before daylight and heading toward the water hole. They sat waiting for the sun to come up, chewing cold biscuits and sipping water from their canteens. Once it was light enough, Zac led the way down the granite ridge into the valley.

Dan moved to the left and Vic to the right, while Zac rode down the middle of the valley. Within a quarter-mile, the trail was picked up. After five miles, Zac noticed where the Alans had camped next to a spring.

Zac looked the camp over. "They were here for two days, maybe three."

"How do you figure?" Vic asked.

Zac pointed to their trash pile, "At least six pots of coffee were made, and there are empty cans for enough meals to cover two days."

"What we have are some bad guys that are not too ambitious. Just like the last time, they stopped as soon as they could," Dan pointed out.

The three rode hard until dark. The trail was easy to follow and had led them out of the valley. Vic chose a spot to spend the night in an aspen-covered side hill. Coffee was made over a small fire. The meal consisted of the last of their biscuits and jerky.

The dawn welcomed them with gray skies and the threat of rain. After a quick meal of jerky washed down with coffee, the horses were saddled and the search continued.

The rain started with a light sprinkle mid-morning. The cousins put on their rain slickers. The trail was still visible, but Vic could tell Zac was worried. He kept looking at the darkening rain clouds.

The three men continued on their soggy pursuit, deciding to forego any noon meal. It was early afternoon when the cold spring rain began to come down with a vengeance. Within an hour, all sign of the Alans was lost.

Huddling under some pine trees, the cousins planned their next move.

Zac shouted over the roaring rain, "The trail has been going due west. It appears like they have an objective. I say we continue west until nightfall. With luck, the rain will stop during the night and we can try and pick up the trail again tomorrow."

"Sounds like a good plan," Vic agreed. "Knowing the Alans, I think they're holding up someplace rather than ride in the rain."

As the cousins rode on, the bone-chilling rain continued. Their hats were saturated, allowing the cold rain to run down their necks under the slickers. Their faces were numbed by the wind-driven rain.

The heavy clouds brought dusk early. Tired, hungry, and cold, the three trudged on, looking for a spot to spend the night. The rain had stopped, but the cold wind continued.

The area was covered with scattered pine trees and bramble bushes. Zac could just make out an animal path that wound through the growth. He could not be sure they were still going west. He was using the wind direction as a guide and hoped it hadn't changed since the rain stopped.

Dan noticed some light about a quarter-mile through the trees. Gradually, the shape of a low log building appeared. Dismounting, the cousins removed their slickers and led their horses as they looked for signs of danger. Dan checked the stable in the back. There was just one horse.

The building was a trading post. Smoke hung heavy out of a leaning stove pipe on the roof, promising warmth within.

Vic stepped into the dimly lit room. There were several shelves against the back wall loaded with canned and dry goods. The right wall had shovels, picks, pry bars, drill rods, and other items that could be used for mining. On the left was a plank bar. Alongside the bar was a blanket covering a doorway.

There was the smell of leather goods and new rope. It mingled with the odor of sweat and spilt rye.

A short fat man with slits for eyes leaned against the bar. He had a greasy collared shirt, with the front covered with food stains. His oversized pants were held up by well-worn suspenders.

"Welcome to Ham's Trading Post. I'm Ham," the fat man said. When he smiled, he displayed widely-spaced, yellow, tobacco-stained teeth.

The three walked slowly past the potbelly stove, welcoming the heat. Standing at the bar, Dan ordered shots of rye. He rolled a cigarette and lit it from a nearby candle.

The trading post looked like the type of place the Alans would stop to spend some of the Percys' money. Vic decided to do some fishing.

"We were supposed to meet a couple of friends near here and it appears we missed them, Ham," Vic said. "Our friend Sid had some knife scars and Len has a bad right arm. You haven't seen them, have you?"

Ham looked skeptically at Vic. "Business has been slow here lately. I have ladies in the back I got to feed."

Dan paid for their drinks with a $20 gold piece. Ham scooped up the gold piece and quickly made change, which was a bit short.

Zac shrugged, following Vic's lead. "We best be going. Sid and Len will be wondering where we are. Best we keep looking for them."

The three turned to leave and Ham

called them back. "You won't miss them . . . they left a couple of hours ago. Went to the tracks to wait for the train. It doesn't go by until morning."

Turning back to the bar, Ham quickly poured them three more shots. His rye wasn't half bad. Dan tossed some money onto the bar and Ham took what he needed, plus a little.

"I got girls in the back. They are sleeping right now. Your friends kept them up most of the night and day. I can wake them for you," Ham said with a big, toothy smile.

Vic had hoped to get a meal before leaving. The prospect of whatever was behind the curtain was hurrying them along. Though the night outside was cold, the three wanted to leave the trading post and find the Alans.

"We need to go check in with our friends so we don't miss them. After, we'll come back and check out your girls," Vic lied.

"Good, good, good," Ham blurted. "They should be camped less than a mile up the track. I could show you."

"Not necessary, Ham," Dan said. "Start heating some water so we can take a bath when we get back."

Tossing down four bits, Dan bought three cans of peaches to go.

As they rode away, enjoying the peaches in heavy syrup, Zac looked at Dan. "Heat water for a bath?"

"I just hope he uses it when we don't return," Dan smiled.

A half-mile from the tracks, they could see a fire. They left their horses tied to some small aspens.

"There has been enough killing," Vic stressed. "We take these dogs alive and bring them back for the justice of Sheriff Arnold."

They got within a short sprint of the fire. The two Alan brothers were sharing a bottle and kidding about Ham's girls. Len stood up to relieve himself and walked just beyond the firelight. Zac disappeared like a ghost. Dan and Vic crept closer, cutting the distance to the fire in half.

They heard Len cry out, and then there was a grunt and silence.

"Len! Len! Answer me, damn it!" Sid shouted.

He started to move in the direction that Len went. A porcupine scraped against a tree as it climbed just to the left of where Len disappeared. Sid swung his gun toward the sound and fired several shots.

Suddenly, they heard something crash to the right of where Len went. Sid shot several times toward that sound. The starless night had Sid spooked. He began to load his gun.

Dan was running low, getting behind Sid as he shot the second time. Sid looked up just in time to see Dan fly through the air and tackle him. They went rolling in the dirt, causing Sid to lose his gun. Sid clawed and bit at Dan. He was drunk, and screaming something incoherent.

Dan got him on his belly and twisted his arm up his back. Vic reached the two and grabbed Sid's flailing legs. It took a couple of minutes to finally subdue Sid, and only an additional few more seconds to bind him hand and foot.

Zac came out of the woods dragging Len by the collar. Len had a large lump on the side of his head. Dan came over and tied him up and dragged him over to Sid.

Dan sat down, breathing hard. "Took you long enough to pitch in, Vic," he gasped.

It was four days before they arrived back at Medicine Bow. The sheriff looked at the bedraggled prisoners.

"You boys just don't know how to follow instructions. I said bring back the heads," he scolded. "More trial expense for the town."

He pulled Sid and Len off their horses and pushed them toward the jail, "Git on in there," he said.

Sheriff Arnold had Zac, Vic and Dan give information about the capture. He took the $300 from a metal box in the office.

"Here's your money," he said. "You did a good job of earning it."

The cousins looked at each other. "Why don't we give it to Mrs. Percy. She may have a store, but it will be a hard road for her." Vic said.

"You're good boys . . . uh, men. I'll give it to her," he promised. "And I will send a telegram to the Cheyenne sheriff and thank the son-of-a-bitch for letting the Alans come to Medicine Bow and hurt people here."

CHAPTER FIFTEEN

It was the beginning of June when the cousins got back to the stream where grandpa had tracked Jed. It was less than four days from the green valley. After two days of following the stream, Zac pointed to the sun-bleached skull of a horse. Further investigation revealed some stones that could have been the grave of Jed. The stones were scattered into an oval like something had routed out whatever was under them.

If this discovery was correct, it was just two days to the green valley. Vic suggested traveling several miles west of the site where Jed was killed. The notes in the ledger were quite graphic about what had happened to Jed. Just in case his tortured spirit was still around, he wanted distance.

It was late morning when they saw an

opening in the granite cliffs that could be the mouth of the valley. Their route had been along the stream on the high plains and there was plenty of early summer grass for the horses. The wild flowers were in full bloom. The brush and trees were covered with healthy, young leaves.

The cousins doubted that the valley could be an improvement. The hillsides around the opening were covered with trembling aspen. The slightest breeze made them flutter rapidly, creating a pleasant sound.

Entering the mouth of the valley, they stopped their horses and stared. The men looked in awe, realizing what their Grandpa Oli had felt when he first saw the valley. The floor of the valley was covered with thick green grass. Summer flowers of yellow and purple dotted the area. A cascading waterfall tumbled into a large pond, almost a lake.

The lush green valley ran back over two miles. The hills on the side were covered with evergreens and aspen. Dan led the way to a small cabin built near the pond. It had moss-covered shingles on the roof. A flagstone chimney and fireplace was built on one end. The hand-hewed plank door hung loose on leather hinges. The floor was carefully fitted flagstone.

A rotting cage that had once contained rabbits, or some type of fowl, lay in front of the cabin. A rusty axe with a broken handle lay near a decayed block of wood. No doubt it had once been the chopping block.

The cabin had two bunks in ill-repair on the wall opposite the fireplace, and a handmade table and two chairs. One chair leg had been chewed in half by a porcupine.

Vic and Dan took care of the horses and set up a temporary camp in the cedar grove. Zac went to the pond to try his luck bass fishing. True to their grandpa's ledger, the fish were hungry and quickly Zac returned with enough fish for a meal.

The afternoon was spent enjoying the fish and making the cabin habitable for their short stay. The two bunks were removed and the table was put next to the wall. Cedar boughs were cut and stacked on the floor to make a comfortable bed.

Clouds built up in the evening sky. By midnight, it started raining. The cedar boughs had to be moved a bit to avoid the leaks in the roof. For two days it rained steadily. It was depressing sitting in the cabin, staring at the gray skies. The cousins were anxious to move north and start searching for the gold.

The horses didn't seem to mind the rain while grazing on the thick green grass. Their picket location was moved each day. Occasionally, a head would rise, looking down the valley at the elk or when the tom turkeys would challenge rivals for their hens.

Dan woke as the light was just coming to the eastern sky. He didn't hear the rain dripping. The morning was cool and damp. He got the cooking fire going in the flagstone fireplace and stepped out into the freshest air he had ever smelled. The chestnut whinnied to him.

Dan poked his head back into the cabin and let the others know he was going to ride down the valley. Soon, the chestnut was saddled and Dan rode past the pond. He had never seen beauty to match this in all his travels. The granite cliffs on the north side were a natural barrier. The foot hills on the west and south side were tree-covered. There was plenty of material for building a ranch.

Dan daydreamed about having a home in this valley as he rode. A turkey flew up, startling the chestnut. Dan controlled it with his knees and drew his Colt .44. In a fluid motion, the gun swung up and he squeezed off a shot. The turkey's wings collapsed, and it tumbled into a heap.

Dan froze with the Colt in his hand, smoke curling out of the barrel. He had not even thought about aiming at the turkey. He should have been proud of the shot, but he did not want to be fast, or worse, be known as a fast gun.

He rode back to the cabin with the turkey hanging from his saddle. He had made a decision. Once the hunt for gold was over, he would purchase some cattle and start a ranch right in this valley, away from others who might force his hand with a gun.

The cousins rode from the valley with Vic and Zac looking toward the horizon. Dan kept looking back at his future home.

Figuring that their grandpa traveled 30 miles every two days, he hadn't found anything before the Stinking Water River. This helped them to make good time riding to the river. Maps acquired in Medicine Bow of the Wyoming waterways were very helpful. It was hard to imagine their grandpa traveling the same area with only hand sketched maps.

On June 26, 1890, they arrived at the Stinking Water River. Two days were spent washing clothes, fixing equipment as needed, and hunting for some fresh meat.

Vic spent a lot of time looking at the ledger. "The way I have it figured," he started, "our grandpa would travel 30 miles and then search a radius of 15 miles around his camp. He had four travel days after the river. That would put him 120 above the Stinking Water River, just into Montana."

"What are you saying, Vic?" Dan asked.

"What I am saying is . . . the ledger is better than a map. It allows us to skip searching for the next 90 miles. He didn't find anything until the fourth move. We can be 90 miles north in three days easy riding and then start serious searching."

Zac and Dan nodded their agreement. If their search overshot the location by one day, after searching north of the 90 mile target, they could then start working back south.

Zac picked up a venison steak broiling over the fire on a green aspen stick. He took a bite and chewed the tender meat thoughtfully.

"We need to replenish some supplies," he informed his cousins. "We can hunt for meat, but we need coffee, salt, and flour."

Vic looked impatiently at Zac. "I know we are short of some supplies, but we are getting close now."

"Zac is right, Vic," Dan concurred. "The gold will wait for us, and we have lots of good weather left. We don't want to be close and out of grub."

The cousins sat that night, knowing the trip that started almost a year ago was nearing its end. A short delay to get supplies would be a wise decision, in case the search took longer than expected. Sitting around the fire, drinking coffee and talking, none of them were able to settle down and sleep. Well after midnight, they finally climbed into their bedrolls.

The decision was to continue north to Red Lodge, Montana. Coal deposits were discovered there in 1866. An 1880 treaty with the Crow allowed development of the mines. Emigrants from several countries settled in the area to find work. The town had over a dozen saloons and was known for its wild living. It also had the supplies they needed.

The cousins rode in during the late afternoon. Red Lodge was busy. A train was pulling out with loaded coal cars. The engine billowed large clouds of black smoke. Freight wagons rolled up the muddy main street. The saloons were already filled with miners who had worked earlier shifts.

Dan noticed that one of the pack horses was favoring a front leg. Zac checked it and confirmed the shoe was loose.

"We'll need to find a smithy after we put up the other horses."

"When we do find one, I want to also get my bay shoed," Vic said.

The livery was run by a short, potbellied man who had a garlic smell about him. He was quick to smile and promised to give their horses a generous portion of oats. The cousins didn't fully trust the smiling livery man and hung around, rubbing down the horses until the oats arrived.

The blacksmith shop was next to the livery. It was run by a stocky man named Lars. Arrangements were made to have the shoes replaced on the pack horse and Vic's bay. He also offered to check the rest of the cousins' horses.

The thick-armed smithy recommended a hotel. Vic noticed the number of white scars covering the man's tanned arms.

"I see you get close to your work sometimes," Vic commented.

Spitting tobacco juice into his forge, Lars gave Vic a toothy smile. "Don't hardly notice it no more. By the way, while you men are in town you might want to get a good hot soak. It is just east of town."

After getting a room and stowing their gear, the cousins decided to check out the night life. The sound of a slightly out-of-tune piano drew them to a brightly-lit saloon. A long, well-varnished bar ran down the right side and wrapped around the back of the room. Several tables were set up for card playing. The smell of tobacco, spilt beer, and the sweat of patrons was strong.

A large-bosomed redhead in a gaily-colored dress met them at the door, "My name is Sadie, and you look like the kind of cowboys that would be willing to buy a girl a drink."

Vic smiled and looked at her round face, which had too much rouge and eye makeup. "Honey, we are here for a drink ourselves and would be happy to buy you one."

Sadie led them to a table and snapped her fingers at the bartender. Zac followed, glaring at Vic.

Dan looked around the room. A sweating piano player pounded out the tunes, dressed in a stained white shirt and a derby hat. Two roughly-dressed men were standing at the bar and nursing their drinks. Their backs were to the cousins.

Several tables had men playing cards. By the looks of their dress, they were miners. The shuffling of cards and sounds of chips competed with the piano. Several ladies dressed similarly to Sadie worked the tables.

The rye was better than average. Zac chose a mug of beer. Several of the card players directed angry looks at Zac. Little Big Horn and the Indian wars were not far enough back to make them forget.

Sadie leaned close to Vic and began to nuzzle his ear. He could smell the cheap perfume mixed with her sweat.

"You looking for some fun tonight?" she whispered. "I got a nice, soft bed upstairs."

Vic moved away, his face bright red. "Your offer is tempting, Sadie, but we haven't had our supper yet and need to get an early start tomorrow."

She tossed down her drink and looked at the smiling faces of Dan and Zac. Snorting, she shoved Vic and, uttering an obscenity, she moved on to greener pastures.

"You sure know how to attract them," Dan kidded Vic.

The next morning, they dropped a list off at the mercantile and headed for the bath house. It had been a long time since the saunas of Elkader, and a hot soak sounded good.

"It sure beats washing up in a cold creek," Zac said, sitting neck deep in the large tin tub.

"You might even be able to get Sadie's perfume off your ear," Dan teased Vic.

"Enough about Sadie already," Vic retorted, "but I think I will soak that side of my head a bit."

The bath house was run by a Chinese family. Laundering of clothes was also offered. The tubs were filled with hot mineral water and felt great. It helped to wash away the memories of all the cold baths on the trail.

A middle-age lady gave shaves for two bits each. Each took advantage of her sharp razor and deft hands. Vic rubbed his hand over his shaved cheek. He had never experienced a shave that felt as smooth.

Refreshed from the bath, the cousins dressed in their extra long johns and trousers. Dan noticed that his extra shirt was threadbare, and decided that he would pick up a new one before leaving town.

Sitting and waiting for their clothes to dry, Vic sniffed the air. The good smell of something cooking was in the air. He noticed the Chinese squatting down and stirring something in a pan that looked like it should be used for panning gold.

An old, wrinkled man with a long braid

turned to the cousins. "You want some? We cook for you."

While their clothes dried, they enjoyed their first stir fry meal. Each was given a bowl of tan-colored rice and two sticks to eat with. The chopsticks were quickly set aside and the cousins scooped the stir fry and rice with their fingers.

The Chinese were chuckling at the way they were eating, but the fare was good and the cousins feared they would starve before learning to eat with the chopsticks.

They decided to spend one more night in town sleeping in comfortable beds. The horses had their shoes fixed and could use another day's rest and oats.

The cousins stayed clear of the saloon. None of them wanted to have to wash off Sadie's perfume. The hotel clerk recommended a small café that served a hearty supper.

Pretty's Café served them generous pieces of roast beef, with plenty of potatoes and green peas. The young lady who brought supper was much more enjoyable to be around than Sadie.

"We have berry pie for dessert," she let them know.

Vic was taking his last bite of the pie when two rough-looking men he had seen in the saloon came in. They sat at a table across the room and began to talk in low voices.

RETURN TO OLI'S GOLD

The sun was going down when the cousins left the café, bellies full of good food, buttermilk, and coffee to wash the pie down.

Clouds were coming over the mountains as they walked into the hotel. It was mid-July 1890. Vic stopped for a moment to look at the faded posters about Montana becoming a state. It had happened nine months ago. He realized how fast time passes. It was time to continue looking for the gold.

The first day's riding was done in a misty rain. Their rain slickers did a serviceable job of keeping them dry. That night, camp was set up in a stand of lodge pole pines. The long, wet day's ride had the cousins exhausted. A quick supper was eaten after rubbing down the horses and picketing them. Then, using the slickers as a top cover, they turned in early.

Vic woke before sunrise. He lay with his eyes closed, listening to the early morning sounds. Large drops of water were dripping from the pines. A mourning dove was cooing in the distance. The doves were sometime called rain doves. Vic figured that was fitting, with the wet day experienced yesterday.

The eastern sky was not yet getting light. He could hear the even breathing of Zac and Dan. He lay huddled in his covers and thought back to the past year, about leaving the family he had known in Elkader. Vic wondered if he would ever travel that way again. The pain of the loss of Grandma Joan was still strong. Carla had been one of the joys of the trip. Now she was gone, possibly out of his life forever.

Vic heard Zac groan. Looking over, he saw that Zac was sitting up. It was time to have breakfast and continue the search.

The next two days were bright and sunny. They arrived in the area, estimated to be 90 miles north of the Stinking Water River, ready to start the search. To cover more area, each would search a different direction to the north, west and south.

The objective was to investigate all canyons, while looking for the low hills with a double peak on the left and a rounded peak on the right.

Zac returned the second day and noticed some strange horses as he rode in. He saw three men talking to Dan and Vic. Dan saw him coming in and quickly stood and turned to Zac.

"Any luck tracking the deer?" he called.

Zac hesitated a moment while dismounting. He thought, *What deer?* Suddenly, he realized that Vic and Dan had come up with a reason to be here in the foothills.

"I trailed it over the hill back yonder. I lost it about a mile beyond," he replied.

He kept himself busy while listening to

the conversation at the fire. It was soon revealed that the three men were fly fishing. They were working the streams around the Yellowstone. There was talk of staying around and sharing the camp.

Zac walked up with his saddle. "If you want good fly fishing, I would recommend you try the Clark's Fork off the Yellowstone River."

Zac drew a sketch in the dirt. He talked of the rapids and seeing large trout jumping for insects on the water. He watched as the three men's eyes lit up. He continued telling them about some mountain streams that drained into Clark's Fork, and the possibility of good fishing in them.

Early the next morning, the three strangers packed up and left. They were heading for Clark's Fork with visions of great fishing.

"I darn near joined them, you made it sound so good," Dan kidded Zac.

It was time to move the search north 10 more miles. Again, two days were spent steadily working their way through the foothills and canyons. This type of move was repeated twice more. After the last move, while setting up camp, Vic stood and made an announcement.

"We will find the gold from this camp."

"Why all the confidence, Vic?" Zac inquired.

Vic pointed to a stand of trees. "Those are beechnut trees. Grandpa was eating beechnuts when he found the gold."

While roasted antelope steaks, they watched the bean pot bubble. The sounds in the foothills were relaxing. Birds could be heard feeding their young, and foxes yapped as they hunted for mice in the plains grass. Every puff of breeze caused the aspen leaves to tremble.

Each man knew that he was on the same trail as their grandpa. The only difference was that they had good horses and plenty of food. And most importantly, winter wasn't around the corner. Vic made biscuits in the Dutch oven, to be eaten with honey poured over them.

Zac was searching north of the camp. He broke out of the aspen-covered hillside. In front of him were two sets of horse tracks. Zac could see that the riders had followed an old trail leading into a canyon. He moved cautiously, watching for any sign of the horsemen. He stopped the piebald and stared in disbelief at the hills beyond the canyon. The one on the left had two jagged peaks and the one on the right had a round top. The other thing he noticed was a smoke trail rising between the two hills.

"Darn lot of men wandering in this wilderness," he muttered.

Pulling off the trail, Zac left the piebald

tied to some low bushes. He moved as quietly as a mist through the aspen-covered hills. He worked his way to the edge of the canyon. From his vantage point, Zac could not see another exit from the canyon. Near the center, two men had set up camp. A pool of water next to the edge of the canyon wall offered plenty to drink.

Zac was concerned. It appeared that the two men had been in the valley for some time. He slowly scanned the rest of the canyon. He could see mounds that might have been the graves of the Spanish soldiers. He tried to get closer to the mounds to make sure, but the cliff's edge was shale, and too fragile. The noise of falling rock would alert the two sitting by the fire.

Zac arrived back at their camp. Dan was collecting wood to be burnt later. Vic was preparing their evening meal. The main course was beans, venison, and wild onion soup. There were biscuits baking in the Dutch oven.

"I found something," Zac called. "Let me take care of my horse first."

Dan came running in with an armload of wood. He tossed them next to the fire and turned to Vic. "Did he say he found something?"

Vic tasted the soup with a large wooden spoon, "Yup. Could you taste this and let me know if it has enough salt?"

Dan gave Vic an exasperated look.

Vic handed him some soup to taste. "I told you we were in the area. When Zac comes back, he will prove I'm right."

Zac came walking back and found both cousins watching him, anxiously awaiting his news.

"I found the canyon with the two jagged peaks and the round hill," he started. "I also found two men camping in the middle of the canyon. It appears the campers have been there a while."

Dan and Vic stood with mouths open, staring at Zac.

"That can't be, Zac. I have studied the ledger and the canyon doesn't offer anything that would make someone want to stay there," Vic exclaimed.

Dan sat down heavily on a log next to the fire. "Unless someone didn't want to be seen. It would be a great place to hide out."

Zac sat on the log next to Dan. He watched as Vic busied himself stirring the soup.

"We have time," Vic concluded. "We can wait them out."

"That's true," Dan agreed. "In the meantime, we can keep watch on the trail in and out of the canyon."

Zac picked up his bowl, "That's the plan, then. Vic, you are stirring the soup to mush. You might check those biscuits, they smell good. I think I will try your soup."

The three ate the thick bean and venison soup. Dan broke a hot biscuit into his bowl and mixed it with his soup. Zac got up when the coffee water started boiling and added grounds to the pot.

"I will show the two of you how to get to the canyon in the morning," Zac said as he splashed a little cold water into the pot to settle the coffee grounds.

"We should each watch the trail in four-hour shifts," Dan added. "We can start at daylight. If they leave in the night, we will find their fresh tracks."

CHAPTER SIXTEEN

Vic lay on the aspen-covered hill, watching the canyon entrance. He was just under a quarter of a mile from the end of their search. Two hawks glided on the warm updraft above him as they watched the plain for any careless rabbit or unsuspecting rodent.

He heard horses coming from the east. His first thought was that Dan and Zac were coming to tell him something. Vic frowned that they weren't being quieter. He looked and saw the horsemen. They were not his cousins. These were strangers, and they were coming from a direction that left him exposed.

Vic flattened himself behind a small windfall. He did not worry about his horse. It was tied behind the hill, well out of sight. The two men were dressed for living off the back of a horse. Their pants and shirt were worn wool. They had wide floppy hats, neckerchiefs, and leather vests. Their boots were worn, and their saddles had bedrolls and saddlebags.

Vic realized that he had seen the men before, in Red Lodge. The two were well-armed, with rifles in their saddle scabbards and tied-down guns on their hips. The riders trotted up the canyon trail with a certain amount of familiarity.

Vic waited an hour before he decided to try and move closer to get a visual on the men. He was slowly weaving his way through the tangle of brush when he heard a shout, followed by trotting horses.

He leaped into a depression made from spring water runoff. He hadn't realized how close he had come to the trail. Vic peeked over the edge, and watched the horsemen ride by so closely that he could have hit them with a toss of a rock.

All four men rode by him. That meant the valley was empty! As soon as the sounds of the riders faded, Vic trotted into the canyon to make sure it was empty. As he approached the opening, Vic saw their camp was still set up. The men would be coming back.

Retrieving the bay, Vic galloped back to let the others know what he had seen. He swung off the bay on the run. He was relieved to find Dan and Zac near the fire.

"They just left the valley. Their camp is still there, so they'll be returning," Vic said breathlessly.

Dan and Zac saddled their horses, and within minutes the three were riding toward the canyon. As they rode, Vic brought them up to date on the two additional men who had come in and joined the others in the canyon.

Arriving at the trail, Zac swung off his piebald and looked at the tracks. "There are two sets going in and four sets coming out. The canyon should be empty."

They rode single file along the trail into the canyon. Dan led a pack horse with tools, for digging if necessary.

Zac was the first to enter the canyon. He guided the piebald to the left side of the canyon, where the grave mounds should be located.

He found the mounds. Something had dug into one of them. No bones were visible in the open grave. There was a stone with three carved crosses lying on its side.

Vic sat in front of the graves and opened the ledger. Their grandpa had sketched the canyon. Vic looked toward the area marked on the map that showed grandpa's camp. He felt a twinge of regret that they would not be able to spend time in the canyon, seeing what their Grandpa Oli had seen.

Dan pointed to a quartz crescent on the

stone wall across the canyon. The three cousins ran to it. There was rubble below the crescent, which looked like loosened stones from the canyon wall. The rubble would have to be removed to find the hidden gold.

"We could use the dynamite to clear the stones," Vic suggested.

Zac shook his head. "If this stone is covering a cave opening, the blasting will collapse it. Also, we don't know how far the men went from the valley."

"What do we do if they come back before we get done here?" Vic asked.

Unconsciously, Dan touched his Colt. He knew what would have to be done. To Vic he answered, "We reason with them first. If necessary, we drive them from the canyon."

Dan felt awkward after answering Vic. If they had to fight for this piece of ground, would they be in the right? They didn't own the canyon, or gold, any more than the men who were camping there. If they had to fight to hold the canyon and killed anyone, it would be murder.

They worked in silence, removing the loose stone, creating a trench between the wall and the rubble. The heat in the canyon was stifling. As the cousins worked, the kept listening for the returning riders.

Their search was widened along the wall. Zac noticed that a crack in the face of the wall began to develop as they dug down.

Their digging focused below the crack. It began to widen into a cave opening.

The men stopped for a moment and looked at the dark space behind the debris. With their hearts pounding and their shirts wet with sweat, the three doubled their efforts in moving the rock.

Vic ran back to the packhorse and removed a lantern. Returning to the opening, he lit it and crawled forward into the cave. The floor was covered with dust that had been sealed in since their grandpa had been here. Vic could see marks where his grandpa had crawled, dragging his toes in the dust. Some handprints were clear in the lantern's glow.

Vic made sure Dan and Zac saw the marks from history before they were blotted out by their movements. At the end of the cave was a stone ledge, or shelf. Covered in dust, the gold sat in neat stacks of coins and bars.

A quick estimate said there was about 250 – 300 pounds. On top of the gold lay a folded note written on a page from the ledger. Vic held it for a moment before tucking it into his money belt.

It was getting dark as the three cousins finished removing the gold, loading 200 pounds onto the packhorse and splitting the rest between their saddlebags. A final inspection of the cave told them that it was now empty.

Their shirts were dust-covered and stiff with sweat. Fingernails were split and hands were bruised and cut. Dried sweat streaked their faces.

The moon was rising in the east as they finished tossing the rubble back in front of the cave. While Dan and Zac finished up in front of the cave, Vic put the dirt back into the Spanish soldier's grave and piled a mound of rocks on top. He then reset the stone with crosses that their grandpa Oli had made.

Before the three cousins left the canyon, they knelt in front of the three Spaniards' graves and said a silent prayer. The gold they now had had been mined by these men.

As one, they rose and went to their horses. Without speaking, the men rode single file back out of the valley. The night sky above them was clear and filled with stars. The moon was almost full and offered adequate light for their ride. The damp night air was cool and clean. Wolves howled out on the plains. Frogs and crickets punctuated the night with their choruses.

The three cousins were exhausted from the effort. The whole night seemed surreal. The full impact that the search was over had not hit them yet. Their excitement had been dampened by the constant concern of being discovered while digging.

Arriving back at their camp, the gold

was placed near the fire. The gear was stripped from their horses and the horses were given a quick rubdown.

Walking back to camp Dan, was the first to speak. "How much is the gold worth?"

Vic had been figuring that out during the ride. "At $21 per ounce, we have over $100,000 in gold."

"That is a lot of money," Zac breathed. "That is a whole lot of money."

Zac's statement seemed to break the tension. They laughed and talked about how they were going to spend the money.

Dan brought out a bottle of tequila that he had carried since Santa Fe. He poured a shot into each man's cup. Toasting their success, the straight liquor was drank down. Gasping for air and shaking their heads to clear their throats, no one wanted a second toast.

The jubilation of having the gold was short-lived. It was quickly replaced by the worry of protecting the gold.

"We can't leave the gold in the open," Dan advised.

"I agree," Zac said. "Let's bury it just outside of camp."

It was well after midnight when they curled into the bed rolls. The events of the day made it impossible to sleep. The men lay listening to the night sounds. It was beginning to smell like rain.

The gray morning light found the three cousins in their bedrolls, with rain slickers spread over their blankets. A soft drizzle fell, saturating everything around them. It was full daylight, and hazy, when the three started to move. Their muscles ached from the frantic labor the night before.

Vic looked at his swollen and cut hands. He winced from the pain as he opened and closed them. He threw his slicker off his bedroll and sat up, looking at the fog-covered plain. The rain had stopped, but everything was damp and uncomfortable. After a short search, he found some dry bark and balsam branches to start the fire.

After putting the coffee water on, he walked into the brush to take care of morning business. He returned to find Zac checking the coffee water. Dan was sitting up in his blankets, rubbing his arms and stretching.

"What does the note say, Vic?" Dan yawned.

Vic reached into his shirt and removed the note from his money belt.

> My name is
> Oli August.
> I was the first to visit
> this cache of gold. I
> followed a dream of my
> good friend Jolly. He
> died of pneumonia the

winter of 1839. He passed the map to me before his death. I have taken only what I and my good horse can carry. My hope is the gold I have taken will be used for good and to improve my life and others. The weather has turned cold and I fear that the return trip to Boston will be fraught with challenges.

I have no one in America that I call family, but I have met many good friends. This may be the last words heard from me. If it is possible, please send a message to Helsinki, Finland, to the August family, and tell them I have seen much and am happy.

If you are my sons or grandsons that find this gold, it will mean that I have died. It is my hope that I have done well by you. Even now it brings a warm feeling to my

heart to think of having a
family here in America. I
expect only good from
you.

It is time for me to go
now. May God guide me.
Oli

The cousins sat in silence watching the fire. The coffee water began to boil over, sizzling on the hot coals. They didn't move. Each was in deep thought, feeling a bit closer to the grandpa they had never met. The birds were singing, large drops of rain water dripping off the trees, the fire was crackling, yet none of these sounds penetrated their thoughts.

Each realized that from the grave their grandpa Oli had put the burden onto their shoulders to do good with the gold they had found.

CHAPTER SEVENTEEN

The sobering moment of reading the note was soon replaced with serious thought about their next move. The pack horses would carry the majority of the gold. Some would be carried by each cousin.

Breakfast was rolled oat porridge, sweetened with honey. Zac made a pot of coffee. The cousins felt jumpy, often looking at the place where the gold was hidden. There would be no peace until the gold was safely in a bank.

"What town will we head for to bank the money?" Dan asked.

"Cheyenne is the most logical town," Vic concluded, "but they sure as heck were not friendly."

"I agree about them not being friendly," Zac nodded. "Now we'll come to town with money.   Maybe we can buy the sheriff's respect."

"Not likely," Dan snorted.

With breakfast done, the three felt more relaxed and walked to get the horses. They stopped short when they saw the four men riding out of the aspens toward them.

Two of them were the men who had been in the canyon. Vic confirmed that the other two were the men who'd come while he watched.

The man who appeared to be the leader wore his leather flat-brimmed hat on the back of his shaggy, sandy-colored hair. His smile was cruel, and punctuated by the missing right front tooth. His grease-stained vest covered a pot belly. The tied-down holster had a clean Navy Colt.

"What were you doing in the canyon?" he growled.

The other three men were dressed and looked as rough. They all needed a bath and shave.   Slowly the men rode forward, widening their front. The riders stopped 15 feet from the cousins and had them covered on three sides.

"We made a wrong turn on the way back to camp," Vic said coolly.

A hawk-nosed man on the right spit a stream of brown tobacco juice. "Unlikely story. We think you were sent to find us by the sheriff in Red Lodge."

"That's right," a lantern-jawed man on the left chimed in. "I recognized you playing with that redhead."

The cousins realized that the last two men who had spoken were the men they had seen in the saloon, and later in the café.

The leader, surrounded by his men, pointed at the cousins. "We don't like being followed. Chasing a reward is going to get you killed."

The cousins did not have a clue what they were talking about, except maybe the redhead.

A pock-faced man next to the leader laughed a mean, raspy laugh as he went for his gun. The four men believed they had three men caught flat-footed and easy pickings.

His gun was halfway out of his holster when he saw Dan's Colt lining up on him as Dan squeezed the trigger. In disbelief, the pock-faced man fell from his horse gasping for breath.

The lantern-jawed man on the left never saw Zac's arm move to the Good Knife. Suddenly, the knife was in the center of his chest. He reached for his gun. He couldn't breathe.

The hawk-nosed man panicked at the sound of Dan's shot. He grabbed for his side arm, pulling the trigger with the gun halfway out of his holster. The bullet went through his own foot.

His horse reared. It was the only thing that saved his life, as Vic's bullet narrowly missed the center of his chest and went through the left bicep instead.

The leader threw up his hands as Dan's gun swung toward him. His eyes were large, and he begged Dan not to shoot him.

As the echoes of the shots disappeared and the plunging horses settled down, three men were on the ground. Two were dying, one had two wounds, while the leader sat on his horse with his arms raised.

"Get off that horse or I'll put one in your gizzard," Dan threatened.

Zac went over to lantern-jawed man and pulled the Good Knife from his chest. The man's unseeing eyes stared at the sky and his jaw was slack. He was not breathing.

Vic disarmed the hawk-nosed man and quickly began to bind his wounds. Dan had the sandy-haired leader drag his pock-faced friend away from the horses. He was hit high in the stomach, and would likely have a long, slow death. Dan felt helpless as he watched the man. He only wished his shot had been a bit higher and had killed the man quickly.

Dan turned to the cowardly leader. He felt true rage flowing through him. "Your men are shot up for nothing. The reason we were in the canyon had nothing to do with you or your men."

He turned away and leaned against the

chestnut. He realized he had never wanted to kill someone as bad as he wanted to kill the sandy-haired leader.

He could hear the leader telling Vic, "I have never seen a man draw as fast as him. You blink and the gun is lined up, ready to split your brisket."

Dan knew a fast gun reputation would follow a man all his days. The west was not as wild as it once was, but there were those who looked to challenge a fast gun to make a name for themselves.

Zac checked the pock-faced man's wound. The bullet had gone through him and lodged just under the skin, between two ribs in his back. Sterilizing the Good Knife with the tequila, he cut a slit and removed the bullet. He fashioned a bandage around the man's torso, putting a folded pad on the entry, and now exit, wound.

"What did you think we were chasing you for?" he asked the wounded man.

Looking at Zac with appreciative eyes, he answered, "We hit the bank in Red Lodge. Didn't get much money. We killed one teller. Hoss thought you was looking for us in the canyon hideout. He worried you might try and ambush us for a reward."

"What's your name?" Zac inquired.

"They call me Pal," he answered, and then began to cough. Some flecks of blood remained on his lips. The bullet must have pierced a lung.

The leader he called Hoss, sat bound to an aspen, staring wild-eyed at the cousins. Every time Pal coughed or groaned, he furled his brow and pulled at his ropes.

The hawk-nosed man's name was Chad. He let Zac know that Pal was Hoss's younger brother. Hoss felt responsible for protecting him.

Vic and Dan walked over to an area with sandy soil. Quickly, a grave was dug for the dead gang member. They did not place any kind of marker on the grave, but Vic did say a prayer.

Standing near the grave, Vic turned to Dan, "What do we do about the gold? If we dig it up and load the horses, Hoss and the others will know we have it."

"We don't load it in front of them," Dan replied, "I'll take the prisoners and head for Red Lodge. You and Zac follow a half-day behind."

"That will work," Vic agreed, "I will let Zac know of the plan."

Zac was concerned about Dan taking the gang by himself. Vic convinced Zac that Dan had the steel to bring the gang to Red Lodge.

Zac and Dan made a travois to carry Pal. He groaned a lot and was ghostly pale. Zac applied a poultice using crushed leaves and bark. These may help the wounds, but would do little for blood loss.

The arm and foot wounds on Chad looked much better, but were also given a treatment of the poultice.

It was mid-morning when Dan left with the prisoners. He told Vic and Zac that he would meet them in Cheyenne in two weeks. That was just to make sure Hoss and his men wouldn't know where Vic and Zac went should they somehow escape.

Vic and Zac felt giddy as they uncovered the gold and started putting it into packs. The gold was glistening in the bright summer sun. They found themselves looking around to make sure no unexpected visitors appeared.

As planned, both cousins put some into their saddlebags. Another portion was set aside on the pack horse for Dan's saddlebag.

With the sun in the afternoon sky, the two cousins led the pack horses out of the aspen and headed across the foothills toward Red Lodge. It was necessary to be careful not to travel faster than Dan. The travois made two easily followed grooves in the sandy soil.

Red Lodge was a three-day ride from their present location. Two days on the trail a horse was spotted across the valley. It was standing with its head down. The valley floor was covered with wild flowers. Zac noticed that it was Dan's chestnut.

Handing the packhorse halter to Vic,

Zac spurred the piebald into a gallop. He was closing in on the chestnut when he saw Dan walking out of a clump of brush. The chestnut raised its head and whinnied at Dan.

Zac pulled the piebald to a sliding halt and swung down from his horse.

"We saw your horse and thought you might be in trouble," he said.

Grinning and waving, Dan put Zac's mind at ease. "Just taking a nature break."

Vic came trotting up with the packhorses. Relief showed on his face when he saw Dan. "You scared the heck out of us. What did you do with the prisoners?"

"After getting Hoss and company ready for travel this morning," Dan replied, "I noticed some riders coming up behind us. Turned out it was the sheriff and a posse from Red Lodge. They had lost the robber's trail and were heading back toward home."

"The sheriff was happy to take the men off my hands. Pal was doing somewhat better, thanks to the poultice. I figure he will live to be hung. Hoss was a bit worse for wear. He made a break for it the first evening, and was running with his hands tied."

"I kind of guided him a bit when I caught up and he ran right into a tree. I believe he has a broken nose and a nice bump on his forehead."

The valley was beautiful, and had a clear stream running to one side. The cousins decided to make camp and rest before heading for Cheyenne.

Zac started putting a fire together for their evening meal, while Dan and Vic unloaded the horses and rubbed them down. The gold packs were heavy and gave a very comforting jingle as they were placed on the ground.

Once again, the gold was covered with brush and leaves to make it less obvious to a visitor.

CHAPTER EIGHTEEN

The sobering moment of reading the note was soon replaced with serious thought about their next move. The pack horses would carry the majority of the gold. Some would be carried by each cousin.

Breakfast was rolled oat porridge, sweetened with honey. Zac made a pot of coffee. The cousins felt jumpy, often looking at the place where the gold was hidden. There would be no peace until the gold was safely in a bank.

"What town will we head for to bank the money?" Dan asked.

"Cheyenne is the most logical town," Vic concluded, "but they sure as heck were not friendly."

"I agree about them not being friendly," Zac nodded. "Now we'll come to town with money.   Maybe we can buy the sheriff's respect."

"Not likely," Dan snorted.

With breakfast done, the three felt more relaxed and walked to get the horses. They stopped short when they saw the four men riding out of the aspens toward them.

Two of them were the men who had been in the canyon. Vic confirmed that the other two were the men who'd come while he watched.

The man who appeared to be the leader wore his leather flat-brimmed hat on the back of his shaggy, sandy-colored hair. His smile was cruel, and punctuated by the missing right front tooth. His grease-stained vest covered a pot belly. The tied-down holster had a clean Navy Colt.

"What were you doing in the canyon?" he growled.

The other three men were dressed and looked as rough. They all needed a bath and shave. Slowly the men rode forward, widening their front. The riders stopped 15 feet from the cousins and had them covered on three sides.

"We made a wrong turn on the way back to camp," Vic said coolly.

A hawk-nosed man on the right spit a stream of brown tobacco juice. "Unlikely story. We think you were sent to find us by the sheriff in Red Lodge."

"That's right," a lantern-jawed man on the left chimed in. "I recognized you playing with that redhead."

The cousins realized that the last two men who had spoken were the men they had seen in the saloon, and later in the café.

The leader, surrounded by his men, pointed at the cousins. "We don't like being followed. Chasing a reward is going to get you killed."

The cousins did not have a clue what they were talking about, except maybe the redhead.

A pock-faced man next to the leader laughed a mean, raspy laugh as he went for his gun. The four men believed they had three men caught flat-footed and easy pickings.

His gun was halfway out of his holster when he saw Dan's Colt lining up on him as Dan squeezed the trigger. In disbelief, the pock-faced man fell from his horse gasping for breath.

The lantern-jawed man on the left never saw Zac's arm move to the Good Knife. Suddenly, the knife was in the center of his chest. He reached for his gun. He couldn't breathe.

The hawk-nosed man panicked at the sound of Dan's shot. He grabbed for his side arm, pulling the trigger with the gun halfway out of his holster. The bullet went through his own foot.

His horse reared. It was the only thing that saved his life, as Vic's bullet narrowly missed the center of his chest and went through the left bicep instead.

The leader threw up his hands as Dan's gun swung toward him. His eyes were large, and he begged Dan not to shoot him.

As the echoes of the shots disappeared and the plunging horses settled down, three men were on the ground. Two were dying, one had two wounds, while the leader sat on his horse with his arms raised.

"Get off that horse or I'll put one in your gizzard," Dan threatened.

Zac went over to lantern-jawed man and pulled the Good Knife from his chest. The man's unseeing eyes stared at the sky and his jaw was slack. He was not breathing.

Vic disarmed the hawk-nosed man and quickly began to bind his wounds. Dan had the sandy-haired leader drag his pock-faced friend away from the horses. He was hit high in the stomach, and would likely have a long, slow death. Dan felt helpless as he watched the man. He only wished his shot had been a bit higher and had killed the man quickly.

Dan turned to the cowardly leader. He felt true rage flowing through him. "Your men are shot up for nothing. The reason we were in the canyon had nothing to do with you or your men."

He turned away and leaned against the

chestnut. He realized he had never wanted to kill someone as bad as he wanted to kill the sandy-haired leader.

He could hear the leader telling Vic, "I have never seen a man draw as fast as him. You blink and the gun is lined up, ready to split your brisket."

Dan knew a fast gun reputation would follow a man all his days. The west was not as wild as it once was, but there were those who looked to challenge a fast gun to make a name for themselves.

Zac checked the pock-faced man's wound. The bullet had gone through him and lodged just under the skin, between two ribs in his back. Sterilizing the Good Knife with the tequila, he cut a slit and removed the bullet. He fashioned a bandage around the man's torso, putting a folded pad on the entry, and now exit, wound.

"What did you think we were chasing you for?" he asked the wounded man.

Looking at Zac with appreciative eyes, he answered, "We hit the bank in Red Lodge. Didn't get much money. We killed one teller. Hoss thought you was looking for us in the canyon hideout. He worried you might try and ambush us for a reward."

"What's your name?" Zac inquired.

"They call me Pal," he answered, and then began to cough. Some flecks of blood remained on his lips. The bullet must have pierced a lung.

The leader he called Hoss, sat bound to an aspen, staring wild-eyed at the cousins. Every time Pal coughed or groaned, he furled his brow and pulled at his ropes.

The hawk-nosed man's name was Chad. He let Zac know that Pal was Hoss's younger brother. Hoss felt responsible for protecting him.

Vic and Dan walked over to an area with sandy soil. Quickly, a grave was dug for the dead gang member. They did not place any kind of marker on the grave, but Vic did say a prayer.

Standing near the grave, Vic turned to Dan, "What do we do about the gold? If we dig it up and load the horses, Hoss and the others will know we have it."

"We don't load it in front of them," Dan replied, "I'll take the prisoners and head for Red Lodge. You and Zac follow a half-day behind."

"That will work," Vic agreed, "I will let Zac know of the plan."

Zac was concerned about Dan taking the gang by himself. Vic convinced Zac that Dan had the steel to bring the gang to Red Lodge.

Zac and Dan made a travois to carry Pal. He groaned a lot and was ghostly pale. Zac applied a poultice using crushed leaves and bark. These may help the wounds, but would do little for blood loss.

The arm and foot wounds on Chad looked much better, but were also given a treatment of the poultice.

It was mid-morning when Dan left with the prisoners. He told Vic and Zac that he would meet them in Cheyenne in two weeks. That was just to make sure Hoss and his men wouldn't know where Vic and Zac went should they somehow escape.

Vic and Zac felt giddy as they uncovered the gold and started putting it into packs. The gold was glistening in the bright summer sun. They found themselves looking around to make sure no unexpected visitors appeared.

As planned, both cousins put some into their saddlebags. Another portion was set aside on the pack horse for Dan's saddlebag.

With the sun in the afternoon sky, the two cousins led the pack horses out of the aspen and headed across the foothills toward Red Lodge. It was necessary to be careful not to travel faster than Dan. The travois made two easily followed grooves in the sandy soil.

Red Lodge was a three-day ride from their present location. Two days on the trail a horse was spotted across the valley. It was standing with its head down. The valley floor was covered with wild flowers. Zac noticed that it was Dan's chestnut.

Handing the packhorse halter to Vic,

Zac spurred the piebald into a gallop. He was closing in on the chestnut when he saw Dan walking out of a clump of brush. The chestnut raised its head and whinnied at Dan.

Zac pulled the piebald to a sliding halt and swung down from his horse.

"We saw your horse and thought you might be in trouble," he said.

Grinning and waving, Dan put Zac's mind at ease. "Just taking a nature break."

Vic came trotting up with the packhorses. Relief showed on his face when he saw Dan. "You scared the heck out of us. What did you do with the prisoners?"

"After getting Hoss and company ready for travel this morning," Dan replied, "I noticed some riders coming up behind us. Turned out it was the sheriff and a posse from Red Lodge. They had lost the robber's trail and were heading back toward home."

"The sheriff was happy to take the men off my hands. Pal was doing somewhat better, thanks to the poultice. I figure he will live to be hung. Hoss was a bit worse for wear. He made a break for it the first evening, and was running with his hands tied."

"I kind of guided him a bit when I caught up and he ran right into a tree. I believe he has a broken nose and a nice bump on his forehead."

The valley was beautiful, and had a clear stream running to one side. The cousins decided to make camp and rest before heading for Cheyenne.

Zac started putting a fire together for their evening meal, while Dan and Vic unloaded the horses and rubbed them down. The gold packs were heavy and gave a very comforting jingle as they were placed on the ground.

Once again, the gold was covered with brush and leaves to make it less obvious to a visitor.

CHAPTER NINETEEN

Rod Tilison insisted that he be allowed to host a double wedding on the ranch. Carla and Mary went on a shopping trip to Cheyenne. Dan gave his future bride some money to purchase her dress and a suit for him. Carla told Vic she would bring him one back.

The two cousins stood near the barn and watched the wagon driven by Ling. A second wagon followed, driven by Pep. They waved to the girls riding on the seat next to the cook. Rod came from the ranch house. "I need to move some cattle from the open range in the west closer to the ranch. We've been losing young stock from that area. You boys won't be doing anything for the next few days, so you might as well catch up a couple of horses and come with me."

The cousins saddled a couple of mustangs from the corral behind the barn. Rod Tilison brought a tall black from a stall in the barn. He led the way west toward the cattle. Dan rode up alongside the ranch owner.

"I plan to purchase some cattle and drive them to a valley my grandfather had found. I would like to buy them from you, Rod."

"From me?," the rancher said. "I just finished shipping cattle to market before you got back. Right now I really don't have enough stock to spare."

Disappointed, Dan replied, "I understand. Could you recommend a place that I might be able to get cattle?"

"When we get back, I will check around for you." Smiling, Rod Tilison said, "I am sure we will be able to find all the cows you want to buy."

Dan had read about the tensions between the large ranchers and smaller ones. Strain had been put on the grazing area due to dry summers and harsh winters. Tensions that had developed had caused the death of some owners and one woman had even been hung along with her husband. Bringing a herd north to the green valley would get him away from the conflict.

By mid-afternoon the men had the cattle rounded up and headed back toward the ranch. Vic had commented to Dan that he agreed, there were few young stock. The rancher had warned the cousins to be alert for any danger.

Leaving the cattle in the pasture south of the ranch, the men headed back to the barn. Smoke was coming from the pipe of the cook shack. "The women are back," Vic exclaimed.

Shaking his head, the rancher said, "That's Wally making supper. When Ling and Pep are gone to Cheyenne getting supplies, Wally takes over the cooking."

It was another week before the wedding. It was a regular country dance. The two wagons had come back loaded with things for the ceremony, including three musicians, their instruments, and a preacher. The cousins volunteered to work with the crew moving cattle to get away from the frantic planning and setting up of the weddings. Ling was in charge of getting things ready and rushed around giving instructions to those that didn't have a reason to get away.

Dressed in his new suit, Vic stood in the cook shack. He looked at Dan fidgeting in his new suit. "Itchy aren't they?"

Looking at the large crowd gathered to witness the ceremony, Dan frowned. "I want nothing more than to be married to Mary, but I always figured it would be small, with maybe you and Zac."

"I wish the folks from Elkader could be

here," Vic said with regret. "Of course, that would have made the crowd much bigger."

"Carla told Mary that there would be pictures for us to send back to Elkader," Dan said. "The fellow taking pictures has something they call an Eastman."

"Never had a picture taken before," Vic replied.

Pep came to the cook shack. "Time to go."

Dan stood next to the preacher, his heart pounding. Vic standing on the other side of the preacher stood smiling from ear to ear. *How could he be so calm.* Dan wondered.

Their brides walked up the center aisle, stunning in their new dresses. The musicians played while the women slowly approached their future husbands.

* * *

Dan awoke, the morning sun shining through the window. His mouth was dry and his head ached slightly. Next to him, Mary lay, her brown hair spread over the pillow, her hip touching his side. He lay still looking at his new wife. Inside he felt worry and guilt.

Mary deserved to live in a beautiful home with family around. The money he had gotten from the gold could provide this. If they went back to Elkader, there would be a job for him in the sawmill that would provide a good living. Dan had seen women that lived on the frontier. The remoteness and heavy work hardened them. Would life in the green valley rob the warmth from his wife?

Memories of Mary's eyes shining last night as they danced to the music and were toasted by Carla's father made him smile. He wished he hadn't had quite as much to drink, but it sure helped his nerves. After a long evening of merriment, he and Mary had retired to their room. The warmth of her in his arms would be something he would never forget.

Dan looked over into Mary's hazel eyes. She smiled and said, "Good morning husband. Let's get some breakfast."

They came downstairs to find Vic and Carla already drinking coffee. "We were just about to give up on you two," Vic kidded.

"I'm sorry, we had a long night," Mary apologized.

"I imagine you did," Carla replied, a coy smile on her face. Dan just blushed bright red.

By the time breakfast was over, they were all laughing about the funnier things that had happened at the reception. Everyone was looking forward to seeing the pictures that were taken right after the vows were finished.

Setting his empty cup into the saucer,

Vic said, "Carla and I plan to spend the winter here at the ranch. Rod wants to go east while we take care of the ranch."

"We still plan on going to Idaho next summer," Carla added.

"I have been thinking that Mary and I should consider going back to Elkader," Dan informed the group. "We both have family there and my father could use help at the mill."

"Elkader!" Vic exclaimed. "All you have ever done is talked of ranching in the green valley."

"It's not just about what I want," Dan replied. "Mary and I will be raising our family."

Mary sat quietly as her husband spoke. The cousins headed outside while their brides cleared the table. The sun was bright and a stiff breeze swept the grassy plain. The last of the items from the wedding were being cleared and loaded into the wagons.

"Good morning," Ling said, a broad smile on his face. The cousins waved to him and headed for the main barn. Vic wanted to ride out and check on some waterholes. As they were walking into the large double door, Dan heard Mary call him.

"I'll get the horses ready," Vic offered. "You go see what your new wife wants."

Mary had taken a seat on the bench swing. The wind was blowing her brown hair.

As Dan walked closer, he noticed that she was not smiling.

"Vic and I are going to check some of the waterholes," he told her.

Taking a seat on the bench, it was obvious that Mary had something on her mind. "I want to talk about what you said this morning. I don't remember you ever wanting to settle in Elkader."

"Well, up until now I have just been thinking about myself. It wouldn't be fair do drag you far from folks facing the loneliness and dangers that frontier living brings," he explained.

"Am I to understand that if we owned a ranch, you wouldn't be there?"

Confused by her response, Dan replied, "I don't understand what you are saying."

"If I had wanted the security of Elkader, I could have followed the path my sister Marie took. I have always been attracted by your desire to see new places, to travel west. Your father and uncles have talked about the green valley all my life. They described it as one step away from heaven." She paused for a moment before continuing.

"Last night I went to bed with a man that was on his way to full filling his dream. This morning that same man had given it up."

"You don't understand . . ." Dan tried to defend himself.

Mary shushed him, "Your dreams have

been my dreams. I will never be alone, Dan. You will be there with me. Rob was going to look for some cattle for us. When he finds them, we need to be on our way so we can build something to live in before the snow comes."

Dan didn't trust his voice. The guilt he had felt when he had awoken was gone. Putting his arm around Mary, he whispered, "Okay."

Vic stood with the horses waiting for his cousin. He swung into the saddle, as Dan got up from the swing and walked toward him. Soon they were riding to the first waterhole. The two men rode in silence for a while.

Finally, Vic asked, "Well?"

"Oh," Dan said matter-of-factly, "I need to look for some cows."

* * *

That evening Rod told Dan that a rancher near the Red Buttes had some cattle to sell. The ranch was in Bessemer, just southwest of Casper. Once again, Rod tried to convince them to stay the winter at the Tilison ranch, but Dan declined, being anxious to head for the green valley.

Pep was bringing the items borrowed for the wedding back to Cheyenne. Dan rode the chestnut and Mary rode on the wagon.

Tears were shed by the women as they said goodbye. Dan himself had a lump in his throat, but he shook Vic's hand and promised they would get together again soon.

The train station in Cheyenne was bustling. Dan packed his Colt and holster in their luggage. The rifle was in a leather carrying case. The trip to Casper by horseback would have taken almost a week. By train they would be there in just over 12 hours.

The green valley would take two to three days by wagon. Dan hoped to be able to hire a couple of drovers to help with the cattle he planned to buy. The train left the station at 8:00 AM, on the 6th of September, with Dan and his wife starting their future together. Closing his eyes, the sound of the wheels on the rails brought back memories of the train trip from Elkader west. It seemed like a lifetime ago.

It was dark when they arrived in Casper. Music could be heard from the Casper Saloon, light spilling out onto the dusty street from the lanterns inside. Dan led the chestnut down the wooden ramp. Mary waited below, next to their luggage and gear.

"We best try and find a place to spend the night," he told his wife.

All of their worldly belongings sat at the end of the rail station platform. While it lacked many things they would still need to get, it was too much for the two of them and the horse to carry.

"I guess we should have thought twice before accepting all the gifts we received at the wedding," Mary said, looking forlornly at the stack.

"Once we are settled in, you will be happy to have them," Dan replied. "I'll see if the station manager can recommend someone with a wagon."

A stocky man with thinning hair was arguing with the manager about some items that were expected on the train. His face was flushed as he tried to explain that he had received a telegram saying it was to be on this train.

"Mr. Hartwick," the station manager explained, "I don't load the train. If they forgot your goods, it isn't my fault. I will send a telegram to Cheyenne and have them look for the bonnets. I won't have word back until tomorrow."

"Damn sorry way to treat a regular customer," the man snorted as he noticed Dan waiting. "I hope you weren't expecting something from Cheyenne."

"My wife and I just came in on the train," Dan replied. Turning to the station manager, he asked, "Can you recommend someone with a wagon to bring our stuff to a hotel?"

"I can send my boy out to find someone

with a wagon, but the only place we got with rooms is the saloon and I don't think you want to bring your wife there," the manager said.

Then he called to the departing Mr. Hartwick. "Bert! Come back a minute."

The man came back and expectant look on his face. "You find my stuff?"

Pointing at Dan, the manager said, "This young man and his wife need a place for the night in town. Could you and Angie help him out?"

Reaching his hand out to Mr. Hartwick, "My name's Dan August and my wife, Mary, is outside watching our luggage. We need to rent a room for a couple of nights while I make arrangement to purchase some cattle."

"Don't you have an extra room at the mercantile?" the manager asked.

Bert Hartwick looked Dan up and down. He had worn the new suit for the trip. "I got a room, but don't tend to rent it out. I wouldn't know what to charge."

"I would be happy to pay you a fair price, Mr. Hartwick."

The store owner's face suddenly softened. "It wouldn't be right to leave you hunting a place to sleep, you being new to our town."

While Dan loaded his items into Bert's wagon, the merchant apologized. "I am sorry you heard what went on in there. Tomorrow is my wife's birthday and I ordered a special hat for her. I guess I let my temper get away from me."

The mercantile was a single-story building. Attached to it was a two-story addition that Bert and Angie lived in. Angie was a portly woman with a quick smile. She was pleased to have company from out of town. Dan had placed their stuff inside the back of the store, while she took Mary upstairs to show her where they would be staying.

Bert had a stable just beyond the outhouse in the back. The two men put the team and the chestnut in stalls. Using a two-prong fork, Dan tossed hay to the animals, doing his best to keep the chaff off his suit. He then followed Bert to the living quarters.

The next two days were a flurry of activity. Dan deposited money into the bank and visited the land office to arrange ownership of the green valley. The elderly clerk spread a map of the range out and asked, "Will you be ranching both sections of the valley?"

Surprised, Dan looked at the map. It showed a second section extending beyond what they were able to see. "Yes, yes it will be both sections."

The Hartwicks were very helpful, supplying or finding thing Dan and Mary would need: Tools needed for construction, a stove for cooking and heating, cut lumber, windows, a wagon and team, and freighters to carry things that wouldn't fit into their wagon.

They also introduced them to Curly Wells and Lars Hanson, two top hands to help with the cattle. Lars was also a builder and could help with the buildings. Curly was lanky, with a stomach that hung over his belt. He had one leg that was shorter than the other. He always had a smile on his face. Lars was stocky and solid muscle. His father had been a blacksmith. He wore a rabbit skin hat and was much more serious.

Mary was left in charge of getting the last of the things needed from Casper while Dan and the two hands rode toward Bessemer to make the deal on some cattle. It was located 12 miles west along the North Platte River. Curly pointed to the red sandstone butte. "That's Bessemer. Folks coming put on the south side of the Platte would cross there to head for the Sweetwater River."

A man named Rex Wilson had cattle for sale. He was selling out and heading for Oregon. The lean rancher had stooped shoulders and a week's growth of whiskers on his weathered face. His ranch was two miles south of the river.

"I figured the railroad would end at Bessemer," he explained. "I was going to make a bundle selling cattle and land to them that was building the town. All the building is being done in Casper and I was hurt bad a couple of years ago with the tough winter. I am too damn old and tired to start building my herd again."

Rex had just over 500 head of cattle. Dan stood in his stirrups looking over the animals. Most were long horns, but he did notice that the Wilson ranch had some of the short horn breeds. Curly rode through the cattle checking brands and looking for any problems.

Riding back to Dan he reported, "They look fit. Several young stock need to be branded. I would say about a quarter of them should have been shipped to market this year."

For the next hour, Dan and Rex rode around the plain looking at the stock and dickering about the price. The rancher had lost all his hands and was in a poor position for setting the price. The open range that Rex had depended on was rapidly disappearing.

After much discussion, the two men settled on a price that was a good deal for Dan, yet fair for the rancher. Most of the cattle were branded with the Bar W. There were also some horses that Rex said were good cutting animals. Dan purchased three mares, two geldings, and one stallion. Curly and Lars stayed and started rounding up the cattle. Once done they would push them just north of Casper.

Dan and Rex rode toward Casper to finish the deal and transfer the brand ownership. The crossing of the Platte near the butte was belly-deep on their horses. This would save Dan some money. If the water had been high, he would have had to use one of the bridges which had tolls.

The afternoon streets of Casper were quiet when they rode up to the offices of the Cattlemen's Association. The stout clerk kept mopping the sweat off his face while the paperwork was completed. The next stop was at the Casper Bank. Walking out of the bank, Dan felt the tingle of excitement, knowing he was now the owner of his own herd.

Rex put the cash into his money belt. "It's been a long time since I had any cash money," he said. "Let's go to the saloon. I'll buy you a drink."

Dan was anxious to get back to the mercantile and see if Mary was able to finish getting things ready for the trip to the valley. "I'll have a drink with you to our deal, but then I need to get ready to drive the herd to my ranch."

The Casper Saloon was dim and felt cooler after the heat of the sun on the street. Three men were playing cards in the back of the room. A fellow that looked like an out-of-work cowboy was working on a bottle at the end of the bar.

"Hey, Lem. Set us up with a couple of

ryes," Rex called to the bartender. "This here is Mr. August. He just bought my herd."

The bartender set two glasses onto the bar and filled them with the amber liquid. "Pleased to meet you Mr. August. You got a spread around here?"

"I'll be driving them to a valley a couple of days northeast of Casper," Dan replied.

Tasting the drink, Dan smiled. The rye had just the right bite and warmed the stomach. The bartender insisted on buying a second round, wanting to toast Dan and the purchase of the herd. Wanting to remain social, Dan took his turn at buying a round but insisted that he had to leave after that.

Stepping back into the heat of the day, Dan headed for the mercantile. Between the deal on the cattle and the rye in his system, he damned near wanted to skip down the street. He waved to Mary, who was standing on the porch, shading her eyes against the setting sun.

The herd didn't arrive north of Casper until the next afternoon. Dan tried to pay the Hartwicks for the room, but they insisted that they had been well-paid, considering all of the things they had purchased. Angie also told them that they were welcome to stay any time they were in Casper.

Rex had nothing to go back to Bessemer for and offered to help drive the cattle to the green valley. He would then winter in

Douglas with some family before heading to Oregon in the spring.

Dan and Mary drove their wagon near the herd so they could get an early start the next day. The chestnut had been saddled in case it was needed, and had been tied behind the wagon. Curly and Lars rode into town to pick up their gear, promising to be back just after dark. They had agreed to remain in the valley and help with the cattle and the buildings. Three freight wagons would follow a day behind, bringing construction material and other things needed for the ranch.

Pulling the saddle off the horse, Dan picketed it a short distance from the wagon. He then leaned his Winchester Model 1873 against the spoked wheel. Gathering up some wood, he built a fire next to the wagon for Mary to start supper. Rex had been checking on the cattle and came back to the wagon, greeted by the aroma of beef stew bubbling over the fire. "Mrs. August, what you're cooking smells mighty fine."

"Well, Mr. Wilson, as soon as the biscuits in the Dutch oven are ready, we can eat," she replied, giving the stew a stir.

With the meal finished, the three of them sat drinking coffee. The stew was next to the coals in case Curly and Lars were hungry. They caught sight of a lone rider coming their way. "Might be another cowhand looking to help with the drive," Dan said.

He and Rex moved away from the wagon to meet the visitor. As a matter of habit, Dan flipped the loop off his Colt. "Hello, the camp," the man called. "Saw your fire and hope to get a cup of coffee."

"Come on in," Dan called back. Rex turned to return to the fire.

"Hold on there, Wilson," the man said. That was when the man's drawn gun became visible.

"What the hell . . ." Dan objected.

"Shut up and keep your hand away from the gun!" the man threatened.

It was the man they had seen in the saloon at the end of the bar. "Do what I say and you might live to see tomorrow. Hand me your money belt, Wilson."

Slowly, Rex removed the belt and handed it to the man. Without warning, the thief fired at the rancher. He then swung the revolver toward Dan. His eyes widened as he saw fire belching from the Colt .44. Struck in the chest, the man fired a wild shot and fell backwards from the horse.

Dan ran up to the man, ready to fire again. Surprised, he saw two wounds spreading blood on the man's shirt. Mary rushed up beside him, carrying the Winchester. "Dan! Are you hit?"

"Dan?" the would be robber asked. "You're that August? Damn." He then coughed and died.

"I'm okay, Mary," he told her. "Check on Rex."

Still carrying the rifle, she hurried over to the rancher. Dan realized that they had fired as one at the man. Mary had already had the rifle on the man, giving them cover, and hadn't hesitated to fire. He dearly hoped that she would never have to do so again, but couldn't help but feel proud of what she had done.

Picking up the dead man's gun and the rancher's money belt, Dan went to help Mary with Rex. The bullet had hit him high on the chest. She had just stopped the bleeding when they heard horses galloping in their direction. Dan pulled his Colt and waited. It was Curly and Lars.

Returning to Casper with Rex lying on the goods in the back of the wagon and the dead man draped over the saddle of his horse, they pulled up in front of Doc Morgan's. Dan helped get the wounded rancher into the office while Curly went to get Sheriff Winslow.

It was well after midnight when they got back to the cattle. Lars had remained to look after the herd. While everyone was exhausted, they were too wound up to go to sleep. Dan spread their blankets out and they sat drinking leftover coffee from supper.

"I saw him demanding the money belt and I grabbed the rifle," Mary said. "I saw him shoot Rex and just fired. I didn't even think that I was shooting at a man."

"You did just right, Mary," he told her. "If I had just shot, he may have kept his aim and hit me."

The next morning, they avoided the subject of the robber. Rex would be some time healing in Casper. It was time to go to the green valley. Dan planned to fix up the cabin they had found first and then build a small barn for the stock. They rode on the wagon, talking excitedly about their future home.

By midday on the third day they drove the cattle through the opening and onto the valley floor. The knee-high grass had turned gold. Dan stopped the wagon near the abandoned cabin. The freight wagons had caught up with them. They set up camp near the pond and a fire was started for coffee.

Dan and Mary sat next to the water with cups of steaming coffee and looked at the grazing cattle spread across the valley the breeze moving the grass in waves. "Welcome home, darling," he whispered. "Welcome home."

Coming Soon

I hope you enjoyed reading *Return To Oli's Gold* as much as I enjoyed writing it. I am currently working on the travels of Tom Franklin, after he and Oli's parted in St. Louis. My goal continues to be writing quality books for your enjoyment. I would appreciate you taking the time to post a positive review. You can do so by going to the books Amazon page. Scroll down to the button saying "Write a customer review", click it and enter your comments.

Watch for future books as they become available. Your support will be the fuel to motivate my writing.

Best wishes and good reading.

Jim